HOW TO SAVE YOU FROM YOU

By

Stephanie Francis

ISBN-13: 9781699695395

DEDICATION

To my awesome mum, who has been my rock and my guiding star. You are the best person and the strongest person in the entire world. I am proud to call you my mum and honoured to be your daughter. I love you very much.

CONTENTS

ACKNOWLEDGMENTS

A huge thank you to my fiancé and soon-to-be husband, Jake. Without you telling me to click submit, this book would have stayed on my Google Drive and in my heart. You are the driving force behind this publication and I cannot thank you enough for listening to me ramble on and show you chapter after chapter.

Helga

Helga sat staring at the computer, mouse hovered over the 'buy now' button, reminiscing on the day her life changed forever.

***

Tony, her husband of 30 years, had died two years to the day and her daughter had just announced that she and her husband were hellbent on travelling the USA in a band called 'The Locksmiths'.

"But… what about the twins?" Helga questioned over FaceTime that night.

"That's why we called," Daniella explained. Daniella has big blonde hair and big blue eyes to match.

That is where the word 'big' stops and 'petite' begins. Her slim figure, despite having twins, made

Daniella (or Dan as she preferred) the target of immense jealousy from any girl she passed. This, of course, made Markas smug and arrogant. Helga and Tony had advised Dan to not marry the twit but she eloped with him after two months of knowing him. And now, six years on, Helga sits staring at his greying hair and his dulling green eyes knowing that he is responsible for this idea.

"We were wondering…" Markas began.

Eurgh, Helga thought. He speaks and her immediate reaction is to find the nearest bridge and jump.

"…whether you'd have them," he finished, and Helga almost spat out her tea.

"That I'd what?" exclaimed Helga, mortified at the prospect. "I'm too old to look after toddlers full-time."

"Oh Mummy, please." Dan always called her Mummy when she wanted something as she always knew it would work.

"And they're not toddlers… they're five," snorted Markas, clearly revelling in Helga's distress.

Helga sat back in her chair. At almost 51 she could hardly look after a houseplants full-time, let alone two children. But still, they are her grandchildren and the prospect of them travelling around with a band didn't sit well with her.

"How long for?" Helga enquired, making Daniella squeal with excitement.

"One month," she replied. "Three, tops."

She sat there staring blankly at the screen and sighed. "OK. One month. And I mean it, Daniella. One. Month."

***

Well, that was 25 years ago. Helga received a phone call around the three-month mark, announcing that they loved the travelling band life too much and had too many fans to possibly let them down and return to normalcy.

"I'm so sorry, Mummy," Daniella smiled, somewhat ignorant of the fact she was abandoning her children. "We will write every day, promise."

Of course, apart from the obligatory Christmas or rather, 'look how amazing our child-free life is' card, this didn't happen. The children were abandoned with only Helga, the orchid killer, to look after them.

She's done OK, hasn't she? The children have turned into strapping children. They are both successful and adore one another and, unlike her own child, they were both very loving and thankful for being saved from turmoil. The children, now adults, always made sure Helga is OK and put them first. However, something just isn't quite right; she's not quite herself.

The advice says to buy this book; the author is very confident so it must be worth a read. Isn't it?

Oh, sod it, Helga thought and clicked the button.

Jenna

The old Jenna used to sit munching grapes and drinking chamomile tea whilst watching documentaries. The new Jenna, however, sits eating Ben and Jerry's Phish Food, dressed in a coffee-stained nighty, watching *Bridget Jones' Diary* after an hour of looking at one-star reviews of a book she wrote during her grape-munching, chamomile tea days.

How to Save You from You was her baby. She'd dreamt about it, nursed it and presented it to society. An early 20-year-old with a thigh gap and an hourglass figure to match, she was confident, witty and downright gorgeous. Added to this, she was engaged to the high-rolling bank CEO, Liam, and living in a big apartment in London.

They met in a rainy park whilst walking home one evening. Liam, being the phone addict he was, managed to somehow walk into Jenna, knocking her flying into a puddle. Laughing, he took her out for a drink and a meal to apologise. Flash forward three years and there was a marriage all women wanted and envied. Liam Ashton was off the market which was a sad day for all.

Flash forward one more year, he is now gone and she is watching Colin Firth punch Hugh Grant in the face, alone.

"You really need to go out there meet someone," Abby, Jenna's best friend said softly over Skype, slightly amused by how much ice cream Jenna could actually eat in one mouthful. "And it's no good you crying over your one-star ratings. There must only be five of them anyway."

"Seven now," sniffed Jenna, who began to move onto the Pringles – sour cream and chive, obviously. "Anyway, clearly I'm crying because Bridget should have chosen Mark from the start."

"Hmm… yeah, OK. Seven out of what exactly?" Abby couldn't help but smile sympathetically. She loved Jenna to bits but she hated seeing her like this. She had seen Jenna deteriorate from being a thin, confident woman who loved reading the five-star comments over coffee to a more curvy, shadow of a woman who hides in her favourite coffee shop answering letters to people in need. Whilst there is nothing wrong with being curvy, Jenna had taken to eating to help her cope with the loss of Liam.

"Well… out of about 10,000 but that's not the point," huffed Jenna. Wailing rang out of the speaker, this time not from Jenna. Abby sighed.

"Bobby is awake, gotta go, love you lots." Before Jenna could even say 'OK', Abby was gone to tend to her nine-month-old baby and the screen went blank, reflecting her tear-stained, mascara-smudged face.

Popping her evening feast wrappers and cartons in the bin, Jenna slumped off to bed wondering why she was so low all of the time. But then again, she knew the answer to that. Didn't she?

Dan

"Dan... sweetie... Daniel," whispered Helga. "DANIEL."

DANIEL woke up with a start, shouting obscenities, and knocked empty Red Bull cans across the floor. Ever since Dan started working at *The Echo News Weekly*, he had been up all hours of the day and spent most of his time in front of his laptop. Now, Helga wasn't a young one, but she knew spending time in front of a laptop light wasn't great for your health.

"What? What time is it?" A confused Dan looked at the clock and before Helga could reply, "Shit! I'm late," and with that he leapt up, ran to the door, paused and backtracked to kiss his gran on the head before darting out of the front door, almost knocking Margot out of the way.

"Charming!" shouted Margot. "Morning, Gran, is Wondertype late for work again? Has he even washed?" Margot, Dan's non-identical twin, enquired.

Instead of replying, or laughing at Dan being called Wondertype, Helga shook her head worriedly and began to clean the living room.

Fifteen minutes later...

"Sorry, sorry, I know I'm late," panted Dan from across the boardroom.

"Actually you're just in time," grinned Sheila. "Have you finished the horse meat scandal piece?"

"Yeah, all sent to publishers," he replied.

"Excellent." She threw an envelope at him. She had a soft spot for Dan, ever since she first stepped into her office. But, as any ruthless businesswoman who has built her business from nothing knows, all interns need to work hard to get to where they want to be. Blood, sweat and tears had always been her expectation and Dan certainly held up to that expectation. So now he deserved to have a serious case, a real case for their readers. After this one. This one may not be big for Dan, but for Sheila? Well, she needed this. A report like this could make her richer and well known all the way in New York! Especially as the New York office made it very clear they needed this specific article. Yes, Dan would do this one, after all, he was the best intern.

Dan opened the enveloped and sighed. He thought he'd have a better report to write about this time. Hadn't he busted a gut to complete all the other mindless tasks and reports? Like 'Aloe Vera: the brilliant plant' and 'Is your underwear stifling your creativity?' But what had he got in return? Another mind-numbing report that would make any credible newspaper laugh and throw his portfolio out:

An interview with Jenna Pace.

Chapter One

S itting in a coffee shop in South Norwood, latte in her hand and laptop on her lap, Jenna read and reread her Agony Aunt blog. She sighed and gazed out of the window; people watching was her favourite thing to do when she was stuck on a response. Watching them bustle by in the rain, snow, sun and all the other crazy weathers the UK is thrown, gave a clarity to Jenna that no other picture, music or scene could.

Just as she started giving the woman in the red scarf the life of a spy, Lionel, a regular customer, sat by her side.

"Good afternoon, Jenna dear," smiled Lionel. Lionel was about 75ish years young, with narrow-rimmed spectacles and an itchy-looking white moustache. Ever since his wife, Evelyn, passed away four years ago, Lionel had been going to the Roasted Bean for a coffee and a chat.

Two years ago, a nervous Jenna wandered in for a flat white and for chatting to Lionel (or rather, Lionel quizzed her on her life) and the rest, as they say, is history.

"And a good afternoon to you too, Lionel." Jenna beamed at her wrinkled friend as her head bobbed to Lionel's mug. "Cappuccino today?"

"Always," Lionel chuckled. "So who needs your help today then? Wife caught her husband cheating with her brother? Man's wig gets blown down the road? That one was my favourite."

Jenna snorted. "Mine too. Actually, this one has me stumped as to what to say."

"Really? Go on, go on." He sipped his cappuccino, foam collecting on his moustache, and waited patiently to hear the letter she had received.

Jenna, clearing her voice, read out the letter with passion, confidence and meaning. Just as he liked it.

Dear Jenna,

I am in serious need of some help. I have been the carer of my grandchildren for 25 years after their parents abandoned them and although they are fully grown I am really worried about them. My grandson is a workaholic. He works all day, eats his dinner next to his laptop and then sleeps for all of 2 hours before working again! I'm worried he is going to make himself ill but what can I do? If I talk to him, he just shrugs it off. To top it off my granddaughter sneaks out at random times at night and doesn't come back until the early morning, sometimes even midday! I don't have the bravery to talk to her and ask where she is as I see so much of her mother in her, I worry what the answer will be. I've always read your blog since I found it on a Facebook ad. You are amazing so please, please help.

Love,

H

Female

From: Dulwich Village

"Poor woman," Lionel sighed, shaking his head. Whilst Jenna did sympathise with the woman, she didn't exactly know how to respond. She wasn't exactly a lazy bum or someone who knew how to stop working, so how could she give sound advice? Sure, she could give advice about men having affairs, etc., as she'd never had to deal with it, but working too much?

Then, she remembered a chapter from her book: 'Chapter 4: Saving others by saving you'. Maybe this would work, maybe. This could help book sales, get more three- or four-star reviews? *Or maybe it'll help Helga out!* Jenna reprimanded herself. She needed to focus on poor Helga who'd clearly lost confidence to help her grandson. *Yes*, she thought, *my book will help*, and she began typing frantically:

Dear H,

First of all, I just need to say this: You are an amazing, powerful woman who has taken time out of her own life to be reborn as a mother, father and grandmother all in one! What a phoenix you are! I don't think many women (or men) would have the strength to deal with an abandonment and two children, especially ones who don't appear to be understanding the gravity of their ways. They are, obviously, adults and you can't do a lot in terms of grounding them and reprimanding them but I do have some advice for you: If you can't beat them, join them!

Now, I don't always promote my book on here, there is a link is at the bottom but I know people reading these blogs already get some sort of response they need. However, there is a distinct chapter I feel that would really support the philosophy of beating them at their own game. They need to know what it is like to be worried and wondering what is happening.

Readers, please do not think I am telling H that going out in all hours of the day and night, staying up too late and working too hard is fine. It is far from it! But a little secrecy never hurt anyone, right? And if it makes them realise what they are doing to you, then isn't that something? Now, read the whole book because I feel it will help you see just how amazing you already are. Look after yourself, focus on yourself because for over 25 years, you have been looking after so many others. I have a few questions for you to think about:

1) Have you done one thing for yourself today? Yesterday? Last week? Last month? Last year? No? Then you need to do so.

2) Have you had a massage lately? No? Then go.

3) Have you gone for a walk and taken in all of the splendours that are in our world? Not for a while? Go now.

4) Have you purchased my book yet No? Then get clicking!

In all seriousness, H, you are a fantastic woman and I really do think you are so strong and brave. Remain strong, remain brave and remain you.

Love,

Jenna

xx

"Don't you agree?" Lionel questioned, oblivious to the fact Jenna had been in her own world.

"Hmm? I'm so sorry, Lionel I missed that. What did you say?"

"Nothing, dear. Another coffee?" Lionel was one of the most patient and kind people Jenna had ever met. She was grateful for the day she popped in all those years ago. He became her first friend in the town. Especially with Abby being in London still, she needed a friend that could make her smile.

"I'd love one but unfortunately, I've gotta head back. I've got five more letters to respond to and then I have an interview." The latter didn't exactly fill Jenna with excitement. It actually filled her with dread. Why? Why did she say yes to... eurgh, what was his name again? Daniel! He sounded so smooth on the phone she could hardly say no, could she? Although when she said yes he didn't exactly sound enthusiastic. First interview in five years; she'd already been sent the questions so the meeting was just a formality but she had already made it very clear: no pictures. No. No one needed their dreams shattered by a picture of what Jenna looked like now, no. She'd rather they remembered her as the carefree, gorgeous woman who walks into a room like she owns the place. *Oh God,* she thought, what a fraud she was becoming.

***

By the time it was evening, nerves had hit her like a freight train. She changed outfits three times and had two showers due to the amount of perspiration running down her face. *This will have to do,* she thought as she flicked on some mascara, her favourite pale pink lipstick from Superdrug and dialled Abby.

"Oh, hey girl! Someone has listened to me and got herself a date, have we?" Abby practically placed her eyeball on the webcam to have a good look at Jenna's outfit.

"It's not a date… You don't think it's too much?" questioned Jenna who was subconsciously stroking her dress to calm her nerves.

"Err… No!" Abby beamed at her best friend. "You used to wear skimpier stuff when you were here in London."

"Well that was before… " she paused, "you know."

There was a brief moment of silence before Abby sighed and said, "I know, sweetie. But you can't keep hiding yourself away. You must be strong and move forward. Move on. If not for you then for your godson who misses you terribly." As if right on cue, a gurgling, podgy-faced Bobby popped his head into view of the webcam. He recognised Jenna's voice and smiled lovingly at the screen.

Jenna flashed back to the day he was born with a smile. He arrived, all 13lbs of him, the day before her best friend's birthday. Naturally, as any parent, Abby wanted her son to be born on her birthday so that one, they could share that special day together and two, to hold the pain and torture that childbirth inexplicably is, to her husband. This would have been leverage for every sparkly and expensive gift Abby would want for the rest of her life. So, as any proud mum would be… she was gutted when he arrived the day before. Although, she still gets whatever she wants regardless of the time of year.

"Hey, gorgeous boy. Oh, I miss you both too, I'll visit soon, I promise. You can always come and see me!" Jenna looked at the time. "Shit, is it seven? I'm going to be late!"

"Go, go, go, enjoy your date," grinned Abby.

"It's not a date, you… pfft! Bye!" Jenna laughed, then sprinted out of the door and down the road.

Chapter Two

Glancing at the intricate yet rusting clock in the Grand Hotel (by name not by vision), Dan had believed that Jenna had stood him up. Just as he was about to leave, he bumped into a woman who, by the red face and sweat flicking off her face as she blinked appeared to have done a workout in a dress.

"I'm so sorry," she huffed. "I'm late for something which I know is no excuse for me being so rude but being late is also rude, isn't it? Anyway, I'm so sorry."

Dan looked down at the crumpled piece of paper he was holding. It had a picture of Jenna Pace on the front so that Dan would recognise her. *This is the girl,* he smiled. *Although she looks less confident and more dishevelled than her publishing picture,* he continued to muse. Astounded by her stress, but unable to help himself, he simply said, "It's fine, I detest being late myself so totally understand but if I could give some advice? Maybe look forward as you run next time?"

"Ooh, you're supposed to look forward when you run. Got it! Thanks," she replied before sulking off to the front desk. "Jenna Pace, I have a meeting with Dan… erm… Dan… Astroid? Avatar? Crap, Dan…"

"Avery," Dan whispered behind her. "You're here to meet Dan Avery."

"Oh, yes, thanks, Dan Avery… Wait, oh God," Jenna yelped, visibly flushed. "You're Dan?"

"Apparently so," he said, tapping his journalist lanyard with an air of arrogance that made Jenna's hackles immediately stand on end. "Shall we begin again?"

"Yes… I think we shall, I'm so embarrassed. I'm sorry, I guess time just flew away with me and well, I was talking to my best friend and her baby came on screen and I totally got sidetracked by his face and…"

Dan, who was clearly not overly impressed by her tardiness or her mindless chatter, walked her to one of the free tables in the lobby. Her hair was practically stuck to her face as she sat down and she was still panting from her run. *Christ,* he thought, *no wonder she dislikes interviews.* She ordered a hot chocolate with extra marshmallows and extra cream to match which Dan found interesting for someone in the literary business to order but decided it sounded too delicious to turn down so he ordered one too.

"Let's begin then," Dan stated at a slightly more composed Jenna, before stating his name into the tape recorder and the title of his article: *An Interview With Jenna Pace.*

"Wow, what a boring title. Could it be more intriguing like: How to save me from this interview?" She found herself laughing at her own joke so much she snorted which mortified her, and Dan it seemed.

"…OK. Question one: What made you write the book?" Dan deflected what sounded like a pretty good and apt title.

"Erm, well I had a good life in Westminster, London. I was helping all my friends with their love lives, their jobs and other personal issues and my best friend, Abby, said to me, 'You are so good at giving people ideas and hope, you should write a book,' so… I did." Dan could see there was some reluctance and disbelief in her eyes but he couldn't fathom why. So he probed, annoyed that the waitress had come over with their hot chocolates at such a time.

"You said you had a good life in London, what made you move to South Norwood?" *Gotcha,* he smirked as her body language visibly changed.

Jenna, who had just taken a gulp of her hot chocolate, cream smothered on her top lip like Dick Van Dyke's moustache in *Diagnosis Murder,* replied rather cautiously, "Umm, well one, my readers don't know I live here so would appreciate that being scratched out of the article."

"Consider it scratched." Dan smirked with a smile that Jenna was not convinced by.

"OK, and the main reason I moved out of London was that it was too busy and I needed time to just… be me." Jenna cringed; was that even believable? Seemed to be as Dan smiled, nodded and moved on.

"So what is your favourite genre of book to read?"

***

After an hour of answering the questions Jenna had rehearsed over and over again in the shower, she realised Dan wasn't actually interested in her responses. Instead, he was more entertained by the ladies walking around the hotel and the men that were clearly there for a good time.

"So what do you do for fun?" Dan winced at the

genericness of the questions, but then again if it was to get him into the company full-time, he'd ask whether she sleeps on her head in a tree. He then noticed a woman he recognised and started to stare. *Why is she here?*

"Well, I love my job so I guess that's fun." *Really, Jenna? That's the best you can come up with?* She argued with herself about this answer but noticed once again that Dan was staring at a woman with big blue eyes and the rest to match. "I also like to run naked in the fields and dance with wolves," she tested.

"Huh? Oh yes, lovely… and are you planning on writing another book?" Dan looked up, somewhat confused as to why Jenna had stood up and got her things. "Where are you going?"

"I've not done an interview since I moved here. I refused as I didn't think I'd be taken seriously enough and I appear to be right. I hope you and that woman over there have a lovely, happy life together. If you can stop gawking for two minutes, send across your questions and I'll email you my answers. Good day, Mr Avery." And before Dan could even open his mouth… she was gone. *Wow,* thought Dan, *she is one fiery woman.* As soon as he saw her she intrigued him but now, he needed to know more. Now back to the task at hand: working out why Margot had a room at the hotel.

***

"Have you been followed?" croaked a voice.

"No, I made sure of it," smiled Margot.

"Then come here and give me a hug," replied the voice. Margot charged in with a smile bigger than her face could handle and sighed relief as she reached the hotel visitor.

***

Dan was sat in his hotel room listening to the tape from his interview and multitasking by thinking about Margot. *Why would she travel almost an hour from our house to this small hotel? Why would she want to even be here and why did she look so shady, checking over her shoulder and wearing sunglasses indoors? What does she have to hide?* Dan smiled. Gran always said he asked so many questions he should be a journalist. Although he was worried he'd blown it as Jenna emailed one-word answers to her interview questions.

I also like to run naked in the fields and dance with wolves. What the...?! He snorted. *How did I not hear this?* Oh gosh, he really did lose concentration. *Well done, Daniel.* He shook his fist in the air in frustration at his stupidity and rudeness. He knew he needed to make it right, but how? He couldn't just email her and ask for forgiveness as that would be rude. Hmm, what could he do? He remembered she mentioned her favourite coffee place to concentrate on her work. With that, he picked up his phone and dialled.

"Hi, Sheila? It's Dan. Yeah, I've got some answers but I would like another few days to ask her some more questions... Yeah, it'll be ready for next month's edition. Yes, I promise. Brilliant, Thanks." Dan smiled; first thing in the morning, he would make it right. He had to, otherwise the article and his career would be doomed.

***

"It was awful!" Jenna exclaimed, rubbing her face with makeup remover. "He must be one of the most obnoxious people I have ever met. So self-absorbed, staring at those poor women walking through the hotel as if they were meat! God knows what he is doing now, probably chatting up that girl. Or worse." She shuddered at the thought and glared at the screen with half a face of make-up, the other half of disgust.

Abby listened to Jenna talk about this Dan character for a good 30 minutes. What was brilliant about having Abby as a best friend was that she sympathised and went through the motions with Jenna, beginning with cringe and ending in anger. But today, that was difficult. Not only because she was exhausted from having a nine-month-old terror baby who hated sleep, but also because Jenna was not taking a breath, or allowing Abby to talk.

"And the way he was like, 'Avery,' like I didn't know his surname." She mimicked his voice and clapped with derision.

"But, from what you said, you had forgotten it," Abby reminded her.

"I'd have remembered it eventually," Jenna moaned. Clearly everything about him just wound her up the wrong way. "And I told you how he looked at that blonde woman?"

"Yes, Jenna sweetie. I know you are very annoyed at this man and rightly so as he clearly was unprofessional, but do you think it's because he was clearly after the blonde girl and not focused on you?" Abby always was the voice of reason, Jenna thought. Was that really the problem? Was it because she used to be that girl, being watched by all men whereas now she was just invisible. Men, who used to run to a door to open it for her, now walk away as it knocks into her.

"No… I just… urgh. Society sucks." She inwardly sighed. "…I'm sorry, I didn't realise the time, you must be exhausted."

Abby stifled an obvious yawn whilst shaking her head.

"I take that as full admission of tiredness. Abby, go to sleep, I'll call you at the end of the week, OK?"

"OK, hun. Just forget about him now. The interview is done. Go back to saving the world one housewife and bald man at a time." She smiled wearily.

"Ha! OK, night you." And with that, the laptop was off and she found that she was actually more tired than she realised and took herself off to bed.

Chapter Three

Helga sat on her bench in the garden and looked up at the old apple tree. She and Tony planted this tree when they first moved in and now it had become as old as she was (almost). She stared at the crooked branches, pointing towards her like a judgemental witch. Its leaves were browning in the autumn sky and the apples looked far from appetising. And yet, for some reason unbeknownst to Helga, she felt safe and loved by this tree. This tree had been with her through all her rough times: the loss of her Tony and the abandonment of Danielle. *But the tree has never left me*, Helga thought as she smiled at the decrepit tree. She loved that tree. It had become part of the family, and a dysfunctional one at that, she chuckled.

She leaned forward and rested her face on her

hands. It had been two weeks since she had sent the letter to Jenna, got a reply and bought the book. She looked by her side at the front cover. Beaming up at her was a thin woman, gorgeous dress and what looked like a very expensive handbag. *What a life to live,* Helga thought. She valued this woman's opinion; a complete stranger was telling her to live life to the fullest and put herself first. That was easier said than done though, right? For years, she had looked after the love of her life and when he got sick she dedicated her time to look after him. When he was gone she had very little time to herself before her grandchildren were left on her doorstep. *Maybe it is time to look after myself,* she pondered, once again looking up at the tree. But she felt guilty. Would it be wrong to start your life again at this age? Would it be turning your back too much on the past? Helga loved her past but she wanted a future she could look forward to. She needed a sign to know it was OK.

At that moment, She looked into the night sky and the stars twinkled like millions of blinking eyes. She sighed once more and marvelled at how peaceful the dark seemed. Suddenly, she heard her front door go. Turning quietly to see who it was, she noticed Margot slowly walking up the stairs. Helga was worried, this was the fourth time this week she'd snuck into the house. She looked back at the book and decided that enough was enough. She was going to do it and that was that.

***

A few minutes later, Helga was in her kitchen. It was small for some people's tastes but for her and her Tony, it was more than enough. Cosy for cooking but spacious to entertain; the perfect match. She always kept her laptop on the island for when she was doing her big bakes or her Sunday roast. She opened it up and went to Google.

Helga typed 'elderfriendship.com website' into Google and had always backed out. But Jenna's book had told her that she needed to push herself; force her loved ones into realising the error of their ways. Not that they were really errors, but her grandchildren needed to realise that she couldn't look after them forever; she was too old for that. So, following Jenna's advice, she signed up for a 12-month subscription:

Name: Helga Garraway

Age: too old

Status: widowed

Bio: Hi, My name is Helga. I have a daughter and 2 beautiful grandchildren. I have been looking after my grandchildren for over 25 years as my daughter has travelled with her band. I like to walk as much as possible and prefer walks in the country than walks around shops! I listen to country music when my grandson doesn't change it to R&B, but I also like Jazz. Looking for someone to go to various places like pottery class or glass painting. Must be willing to listen to me moan and laugh.

She read and reread her bio. "Is that boring? Oh gosh, I am boring," she said somewhat out loud. Convincing herself that there must be other boring people looking for a friend, she clicked save and stared at her new page, thinking about the questions Jenna asked her.

1) Have you done one thing for yourself today? Yesterday? Last week? Last month? Last year?

2) Have you had a massage lately? No? Then go.

3) Have you gone for a walk and taken in all of the splendours that are in our world? Not for a while? Go now.

4) Have you purchased my book yet No? Then get clicking!

Well! One and four are complete! she thought with a smile. *Question 3 I will do tomorrow, the weather is supposed to be nicer then.*

"Gran?" Margot came downstairs in her PJs. "How long have you been down here? It's the middle of the night." Helga could hear the panic and worry in Margot's voice but she knew damn well it was because she was worried about being caught, like mother like daughter.

"Oh, I went to the toilet and remembered I was waiting on a delivery that should have been in today and wanted to check my emails to make sure it wasn't lost," she lied. *How can anyone make lying their day-to-day lifestyle? It's horrific.*

"Ah, OK. Well, I am going to get a glass of water and then going back to bed." *Liar.* "Night Gran, I love you," Margot smiled.

"Oh and I love you, more than you can possibly understand," was Helga's response. "Sleep well, my angel." As Helga watched Margot slump away sleepily, albeit somewhat unconvincingly, Helga couldn't help but sigh. Margot was her angel. For whatever reason she felt like she couldn't tell Helga what she was doing and why she was sneaking around, she would always be her angel. With that, she shut her laptop off and went to bed herself.

***

Elsewhere at the same time, a man was looking at the new profiles that were sent to him on a daily basis. He was looking at the bios and some made him chuckle. Some were confusing and some were odd. But as he looked at Helga's he noticed that she was very lonely. Not in a desperate for friends way, not even in a romantic way – they were both too old for that! But in a 'someone to talk to' way. So he clicked to learn more.

Chapter Four

The Roasted Bean was a steampunk coffee shop. With pipes and cogs dotted around the walls with various sprinkles of bronze, silver and gold tables and chairs to add to the ambience of the room. The smell of coffee hit you as soon as you walked in and the sight of cakes was enough to make the strictest of eaters drool. This was not the reason Jenna was up all the time and was putting on weight quicker than she could eat; night terrors and anxiety were doing their job at ensuring that, but sitting in the Roasted Bean finally gave her an excuse.

"We have a new blend on today," the perky barista, Clarice, chirped from behind the till. "From Columbia, or Canada? I can't remember. Anyway, would you like to try it, Jenna?" She cocked her head to the side as she asked the question, like a spaniel who hears the words 'walk', 'treat' or 'bath'.

"Sure," mumbled Jenna; it was far too early to be that perky, she decided, as she walked her way to her favourite spot in the café.

At the far end of the Roasted Bean was a big, red, velvet armchair. It looked like something Henry VIII would have had in one of his many rooms, a drawing room perhaps. When you sit in a chair of this size and material, you sink and feel safe. Jenna loved that feeling and found that was the only place she felt totally safe, in that little (but not so little) chair.

As she set her laptop off, Clarice brought her coffee to her and squeaked, "Your coffee has already been paid for, so enjoy!" Jenna must have looked really confused, or constipated, as Clarice stared blankly at her before stepping to one side to reveal a man sat on one of the golden chairs at a bronze table holding his own coffee up as if it were a beer and he was 'cheersing' a deal.

It took Jenna a few seconds to adjust her eyesight to realise: it was Dan Avery. *Why?* Jenna thought. *What have I done in this world for him to haunt me at my favourite coffee place?* She raised her mug in response to his cheers and mouthed 'thanks'. He signalled to her that he would like to talk to her and, reluctantly, she agreed.

"Hi," he began. Jenna looked at him and studied his face. She could see the stress of the job was starting to betray itself on his face, crows' feet appearing at the very corners of his eyes. *Although that could be from laughing,* she justified to herself. His hair, slightly greying but nothing 'Just For Men' couldn't solve, however silver fox is in this year. His shirt was from an expensive company, a company she recognised but couldn't remember, a company that Liam… *No, not now,* she reprimanded herself. His look was casual but still smart. What was his angle? Was he working still? Was he wanting more gossip to write about? Then she felt guilty; she had sent answers that were unwritable. *But then he should have been more respectful,* she justified her actions as he said, "I'm sorry."

Well that threw her off guard. "I'm sorry?" she repeated.

"Yes, I shouldn't have treated you so rudely. You are my first official interview, I guess I haven't got the hang of it yet. But, well, my only excuse is that the girl you thought I was… " he paused and shuddered at the thought, "ogling at, well, she's my sister. I didn't understand why she was here in such an insignificant place to her, no offence. But… I guess I got distracted and wanted to see what she was doing here."

"You're telling me this why?" Jenna was shocked by her sharp response. Who was she fooling by being so harsh and mean?

"Because I messed up, I should have explained it to you as it happened. I should have paused the interview and sorted the problem. I should have greeted you with a more professional and polite manner. I was an idiot and I really am sorry, Jen."

She softened at the shortening of her name. Not many people could call her Jen and get away with it. She gazed into his apologetic face. The look in his eyes was as though he was being truthful, although she knew from personal experience that she shouldn't trust a man's eyes. But, she could see the pain in his face, that she suspected was from something else, not from messing up an interview. She watched as he stood there, nervously twisting the back of his hair and sipping his coffee. She knew he was telling the truth; she didn't know if she should trust him, especially as he was still an obnoxious idiot who spoke so rudely. She couldn't trust someone on those traits and first impressions are hard to get rid of after all.

"Hmm," she started. "How do I know you are telling the truth?"

"Because, I came here to apologise. And I know I

could just go back to the office, tail between my legs and plead my boss for forgiveness. I could also make up your answers or elaborate on them myself. But I'm not that kind of person. I believe in sorting problems myself and that is why I am here."

An awkward silence rang out between them and Jenna couldn't quite believe herself when she said in a forced happy or even awake voice: "Fine, I accept your apology." A smile broke out across Dan's face. *Crows' feet from smiling too much,* she concluded, inwardly rolling her eyes at his perfectness. "What now?"

"Well, my first idea was that I would like to redo the interview if that is OK, as the answers were a bit… ummm," he looked cautiously at Jenna's scowl, "unusable."

Jenna laughed. "Yeah, I'm sorry, not sorry about that. I was angry to say the least!" With that, they both started laughing. "Let's start the questions again, third time's a charm, right? Although you said first idea?"

"Yes, I have a much better idea though," he said, eyes twinkling in the hazy lights of the Roasted Bean. "Why don't I shadow you for a few days, see what you do and write about the art of agony aunt…ing?" He could see the fright in Jenna's face, was it a mistake? Should he have been more tactful? Why was she worried or more, what was she worried about?

Panic. Fear. Anxiety. Alarm. All of these words Jenna could use to describe her feeling towards that one question. *Shadow me?* Why? What on earth would he want to know about her life? What would happen if people found out she was a fraud? So many questions ringing around her head. She wanted to run as far from this conversation as possible. Hell, she wanted the chair to absorb her completely. Somewhere she usually felt so safe, was not somewhere she could call safe right now.

"You don't have to make a decision right now," Dan said, sensing her panic and handing her a napkin with his number on it. He had clearly been writing his number as she had been in her freeze of terror. "Let me know?"

And he walked out of the café as quick as Jenna could say, "O…K."

Jenna stared at the number for the next ten minutes. Unsure what to do or even how to respond to anyone. She only managed a nod and a grunt at Perky Clarice and she couldn't even look at Lionel. Eventually, she managed to explain through many pauses, breaths and sips of coffee to Lionel who was desperately trying to understand the problem at hand.

After all, she was an agony aunt, surely she could cope with this kinda thing?

"So… he wants to… shadow you?" Lionel began.

"Yes," was all Jenna could reply.

"And you don't want him to?"

"No, yes! I don't know. Help!"

"Hmm, well it does seem to me you are in a pickle. May I ask, what is it you are scared of? I mean, what is the worst that can happen?"

That the whole world would know where she is. That Liam's family could finally track her down. That the life she loves and has rebuilt could crumble in an instant if people knew she was a fraud.

"He… ugh, nothing. He could be a better blogger than me. Now that would be embarrassing." Jenna produced the weakest, most scared smile Lionel had ever seen. He grabbed her hands in his and simply said a sentence that changed Jenna's life.

"You can't live your life wondering about the tomorrows of the world, just focus on today and how far you have come."

Jenna smiled at such wise words. And she had come far. Hadn't she?

She had built this agony aunt blog from the ruins of her life, rising out of the dust like a strong yet timid phoenix who knew what she needed to do to support her new life. She, Jenna Pace, moved from a city she loved to a town she didn't even know in order to pursue her career in blogging. Millions had subscribed to her blog, millions had written for help. Jenna was a saving grace for many people in the country and she was responsible for all of that. What happened before was, well, horrific. What she lost didn't even bear to be discussed. What mattered was how she responded and that she would have to do once more. *Oh Jenna, he's only shadowing you. Not crucifying you!* she reminded herself. Abby always said she had a flare for the dramatic. "You should have been screenwriter," Abby always laughed.

She looked into Lionel's caring face and could see that he had become a grandfather figure for her. She had no family here or anywhere else that matter – apart from Abby of course, who was a sister from another mister. He had truly taken her under her wing, not knowing her complexities through speech, but he read her in a way no one else could. "Thank you, Lionel," Jenna finally said.

With a huge beaming smile, knowing he had made

a difference, he replied, "You are most welcome, now how about a cup of coffee?" as he waved Perky Clarice over to their table.

Chapter Five

Dan sat at the dining room table staring at his phone. He knew he was a little forward with Jenna but he had tried to make amends, right? He had apologised and she had accepted it. Surely shadowing her was a high form of flattery so why was she so scared when he suggested it? And why did he not get an answer before he left? And why was she not calling? Dan was asking himself so many questions that he neglected to see both Margot and Helga walk down the stairs and join him at the dinner table.

After what felt like an hour of silence, Helga finally broke. "Phone not working, dear?" This clearly caused a fright and confusion for Dan who jumped out of his skin before laughing to himself.

"No, Gran, just waiting on a call." He then

explained to his sister and his gran that he had offered to shadow Jenna Pace and that he would be staying in South Norwood for a few days or even weeks, should she say yes. He didn't go into details of why he messed up his interview, he just said, "I didn't get all I needed."

"South… Norwood?" questioned Margot, clearly distressed at his new potential research case. "Where will you be, um, staying?" The fear in her eyes worried Dan. What was she up to?

"Not at the Grand Hotel, that's for sure, the interview was there and it was a right dump." He glanced at Margot's blank face. "So I may Airbnb it." The relief was visible in Margot's face, well, that was the answer she clearly wanted to hear, much to Dan's annoyance.

Helga, knowing the two very well, knew something was not quite right. They were not the most subtle of twins which helped when they were growing up. But they had developed a level of secrecy from each other that concerned Helga. She found herself thinking back to Jenna's response and decided to give it a go. "I'm going out tonight so you will have to sort your own dinner."

Another silence rang out in the dining room.

"But... you never go out in the evening. You say the dark is too dangerous to drive in," Margot returned in shock.

"I am being picked up." Helga smiled in response to Margot's very abrupt statement.

"By who?" chirped Dan, visibly confused and concerned.

"By a man I met online, we are going to a pottery class." Helga was not only loving her grandchildren's responses, but was also very excited about going to pottery class with a man.

Hi,

I am in my 70s and a widower as well. I was a greengrocer in my day and now a retired man whose hobbies include walking and coffee drinking. I would love to go to pottery classes but I never have anyone to go with. There is one near you in Dulwich Village if you were interested. They are on Tuesdays.

Message if you would like to go, I look forward to your response.

She was smiling at the memory of receiving that message on the website. She couldn't believe that in less than 24 hours, someone had read her profile and replied to it. That was on Wednesday and now it was Tuesday, not a day went by where they hadn't spoken online and now it was time where they finally get to meet.

"But you're too old to be online," quizzed Margot.

"And going out with strangers, Gran. Do you know how dangerous it is meeting people from the internet?" commented Dan, adding to Margot's point.

Margot panicked at the prospect of her gran being taken by strangers. "Yes! What if they want your organs. Or something?"

Helga gave a fake shocked face, then laughed at them. "I'm retired and old but I am not dead yet! And excuse me for wanting a life more than staying in and looking after you. Tidying up after your Red Bull nights and leaving leftovers for you to creep in and eat at any time of the night or day that suits you." What started as a joke had become a slight realisation of just what she had given up and done over the last few years. Years of looking after her own child then her own child's children had finally caught up with her. She was exhausted.

"I am going to go out tonight. You are not going

to worry about me. I will be fine by myself. I can look after myself. Besides, if they want my organs they are about 20 years too late. With all the medication and alcohol I've taken in my time, I doubt they'd want me at the Blood Donors! Now, if you excuse me, I am going to go and lie down. The class doesn't start until nine and I will definitely need to nap before then." Helga swooped off in what can only be described as half rage, half amusement, leaving Margot and Dan flabbergasted.

"She can't just go off with a total stranger," exclaimed Margot. "Like, what if he is a psycho or something!"

Dan realised he had to be the strong one in this. Margot was clearly involved in something that made her too insecure and stressed for her to think rationally or clearly. No matter how much it worried him that Helga was going somewhere that she hadn't been before, with a person she had never met before, at a time that she hadn't been out in a long time. But, like Helga said, she wasn't dead yet and why shouldn't she go out?

"We've just gotta hope that it is a one-time thing, she will be too tired the next day or something. She will be back with us in the evenings sooner rather than later, I am sure of it."

Margot paused and sighed, "I guess you're right. Let's hope, eh? Although she did look pretty excited and you know what Gran is like and… you know your phone is buzzing, right?" She peered down at the table to see Dan's phone lit up and dancing with vibrations.

"Shit!" Dan grabbed the phone and ran outside. "Dan speaking… Yeah, I am here," was all that Margot could hear before the door slammed shut. She found herself alone, in the dining room, worrying.

He would be in South Norwood too. The whole point of going to South Norwood in the first place was that she wouldn't be caught and now he would be there too. That was the last thing she needed, her big brother (of ten minutes and he would always remind her of that) may see her there. What was she going to do? She couldn't move the meeting place, there were no hotels free for long-term lodging for miles, and she couldn't risk travelling further; she was too exhausted from driving there during the day and at night as it was. She needed to go there, talk it through. Maybe they could come up with a plan together. Maybe they didn't need to be a secret anymore. Or maybe this would all fall down and she would find herself back where she was six months ago, desperate and broke. No. She had to find another way, her lifestyle depended on it.

***

"Dan speaking... Yeah, I am here," panted Dan, sprinting to the bench by the witch tree (named by a five-year-old Dan and stuck ever since).

"Hi, it's Jenna? Jenna Pace?" Dan stifled a laugh. She said her name as if she was asking him if it was hers. He didn't understand how someone so blazingly confident, informative and well, bossy about people's lives, could be so timid. He read and saw many interviews when the book first came out and she was just... well... arrogant is the only word for it. Her confidence oozed to the point where she was just so self-assured it was almost nauseating. Yet, when she went off the radar three years ago and returned with a blog, she had almost had a complete personality transplant. What happened in those years? He made a personal note to search for the answer, if she said yes to shadowing, that was.

"Yes, Jenna, I am glad you called."

"Good, well, I have been thinking and I think shadowing sounds fine. If you still want to, of course,

I don't mind doing the interview instead as I am sure you have a strict deadline." Jenna almost sounded hopeful. *Sorry to smash your dreams*, Dan thought.

"No, I would love to shadow you. I want to see what you do and how you do it. I want to find out what inspired you to become an agony aunt and help so many other people in the country." The silence on the end of the line told Dan that this was a response she wasn't hoping for.

"Oh, great. Well we can start tomorrow, 8am at the Roasted Bean. The big red chair and table is where I sit to do my work, I will meet you there. See you at 8am." And she was gone, like a feather in the wind. Dan knew he should be nervous. This was taking a different track from what he was told to do; this was a huge risk, shadowing to write about someone, someone so complex that he thought even Sheila would struggle to get a decent article. No, he wasn't nervous at all. He actually found himself excited. For writing about someone as intriguing and secretive as Jenna Pace, revealing all her secrets to the world, may just be something that shot him up the journalist ladder faster than he could type. He concluded that he was excited for only one reason: his job.

Chapter Six

Jenna hung up and felt proud of herself, well, more petrified than proud but she was trying to remain positive. She took a sideways glance at Lionel, who had resided himself in his favourite spot, next to the window in a recliner chair. He was smiling at her, like a proud family member, then looked towards the window ready to people watch. The Roasted Bean was perfect for people watching. It had the best view of the high street, with windows up both sides of the shop which were tinted so you could stare at your leisure without being found out. Perfect for making up stories for passers-by without them being weirded out by strangers.

Jenna sat with her warm cappuccino with extra foam and chocolate sprinkles. She answered ten letters in the past four hours and began having her much deserved lunch break of chicken and pesto panini with chips and a coffee. Suddenly, she had a video call from Abby:

"Hey girl!" Jenna grinned. "How are you doing?"

"I am good, how are you?" returned Abby.

"I am alright, I think." Jenna began to explain what Dan had said and what Lionel advised her to do. Hearing his name, he looked up from his newspaper, waved, then continued reading.

"So, he's going to shadow you?" Abby questioned, trying to understand all the facts.

"Yes, he is. Why, do you think it is a bad idea?" Panic rose in Jenna's voice.

"No, no, not at all! I think Lionel is completely right. It's just…" She paused to pick Bobby up off the floor, much to his annoyance. "Well you left London, hell, you left your life to make sure no one could find you after what happened. Are you sure you want to open your life back up to the whole world? An interview is one thing, but if he writes a shadow piece about where you go, what you do, will it bring in unwanted attention?"

Mrs Ashton… Mrs Ashton… Can you hear me?

"What? What happened? Where am I?"

"You are in The Royal London Hospital. You've had… you've had an accident. Do you not remember?"

"No, I was driving and then… oh God! Where's Liam? Liam! LIAM!"

Jenna shook herself out of her trance. *Not now!* "I don't know what will happen. I am absolutely terrified of what will happen if this turns bad. But the point is that I can't always hide. I need to show that I am OK, that my audience will continue to have faith in me. Plus, I have a non-disclosure form that me and Lionel created that he must sign before I do this." Jenna smirked. Lionel was the fountain of knowledge.

"Ooh, becoming a solicitor are we?" giggled Abby, jigging Bobby on her knee. "So now we have that sorted. We have something to ask you." Jenna held her breath. She had been waiting for this moment since she heard Abby was pregnant. "Will you be my godmother, Auntie Jenna?" Abby said in a baby voice. Although she had seen Bobby in person, she didn't know whether Abby would choose someone closer to home.

"Well. Let me think… OF COURSE! Ah, it would be an absolute honour. Give my thanks to Jason as well please!" Jason was the quietest and most shy man which made him perfect for Abby's loud and in-your-face nature. Whenever Abby said she was going to ring Jenna, he said hi then left the room. Sometimes he texted Abby to say hi if he was feeling particularly shy.

"Yay!" Abby cheered, raising the roof with Bobby's arms. He giggled as she danced with him which was the cutest laugh any baby had in Jenna's opinion. But she was biased. Until a woman has her own baby, her best friend's baby will always be her favourite. "So, the christening is in three weeks. I know it is short notice but I feel you would prefer short notice than months and months of overthinking. Don't worry, there will be no speech like our wedding was—"

"Oh, thank God!" Jenna interjected. Although she read a speech at her wedding, she was very confident then. Now, she would bottle it and that was the last thing she wanted to do. "It would be a disaster! Three weeks, that's fine. Text me the details?"

"An invite was posted yesterday, you'll get it tomorrow." She smiled back. "Yay, I am so pleased you said yes! Anyway, I best shoot off. Got to sort caterers for the party! Love you."

"Love you, Abs. See you soon." And Jenna clicked the red phone button and sat back in her chair. "Right. Lunchtime is over, I have time for four more letters before hometime." She got up and wandered to grab a latte for herself and a flat white for Lionel who was now looking at art designs.

***

It was 11pm. Helga crept into the house as if she was a teenager sneaking in from a party. *Well I am being Margot*, Helga thought and giggled to herself. She tiptoed into the living room and stubbed her toe on the coffee table "Urgh!" she shouted with instant regret. Footsteps and lights turned on upstairs and two audible adults came running.

"Gran! Gran are you alright?" they both shouted in unison. Unison was something, even after 25 years, Helga found super creepy.

"Yes, yes, yes. I'm fine. Just kicked my toe is all. Honestly, go back to bed."

"Have you… have you just come in?" Dan asked in an attempt to be supportive rather than accusing.

"Erm, well, yes. Pottery class was amazing. See." She held up her pot. "I get to take it back next week and paint it! I am so excited, I was thinking of making it my Halloween sweet bowl." She was so happy it made Dan's heart ache.

"Don't you think it is a bit late, Gran?" Margot

snapped, visibly annoyed she had been woken.

"Well in all honesty, dear, I didn't expect you to be here, let alone asleep," responded Helga in a stern but fair tone. Had she done the wrong thing by going out? She was worried she had pushed her luck announcing that she was going out on the same night as she left. She didn't know. But it was done now so that was that.

"What Margot is trying to say is, did you have a nice time?" asked Dan whilst shooting his sister a look. "And how was your man?" At the end of the day, he wanted to make sure she was happy and enjoying herself. She deserved it for all she had done for them.

"He's not my man. But yes, I had a lovely time, thank you, and he was a gentleman, making sure I got in the house OK. I think he is going to be a right laugh, plus he can't make a pot if his life depended on it." She chuckled at the memory of him splatting himself with clay. "Now, it's late so I need to sleep. Night, my darlings." She kissed both of them on the forehead and limped off upstairs to bed.

"Should we be worried, Dan? After all, being out so late isn't good for her. She needs all the sleep she can get." Margot stared at the stairs that her gran had just walked up.

"I'm sure she will be fine. We just have to keep an eye on her. We know her, that is all we can do. Support and help where we can. Night, sis."

Margot was left downstairs, in the dark and with a huge worry on her shoulders. Should she tell Gran and Dan what she was up to? This constant battle with her conscience was catching up with her. Although she swore she would be secretive about it and that no one could ever know, she had this feeling that if Helga felt half as worried about Margot sneaking in the late hours of night or early hours of the morning, then she was in danger of becoming very stressed and ill.

Chapter Seven

Jenna glanced at her watch – 7.59am. Her stomach was doing flips. She had never had anyone shadow her in a job before. Even prior to her writing career, her accountancy firm never had people shadow her, only work for her. Was that the same thing? She wasn't 100% sure. But she was in clear need of a change and, although she wasn't thrilled about the situation, she needed to ensure she tried.

8.00am and Dan walked calmly through the door.

"Morning. I think this is the first time I've been early for work in a long time." He smiled that melting smile that made all the women in the coffee shop swoon. "Have you got a coffee? Do you want one? My treat."

Taken slightly aback by his kindness, she asked for

a latte then sat at her table ready to prepare for the day ahead. First things first: her laptop. Very important laptop that she purchased especially for her writing job. It had written and sent many letters helping people and if she didn't have her laptop, well she wouldn't be able to function! It was so precious that she watched Dan very carefully place his coffee down on the coaster next to her, before safely placing himself in the chair next to him.

The smell of coffee and aftershave flooded her nostrils and made her feel funny inside. She couldn't quite put a finger on what the feeling meant, so she pushed it to one side and continued to unpack.

The next item: water bottle. It was very tempting as a writer to only function on coffee, tea or any other hot beverage that the Roasted Bean (or any other hot drink shop) could provide. What was difficult, was to remain hydrated and not drink all of one's calories in fluids.

As she continued to pull various things out of what Dan could only describe as a *Mary Poppins* bag, he began to realise just how precise Jenna was. The laptop was at a specific angle, her water bottle placed on a coaster directly behind, the coffee on a separate coaster immediately to the left of the laptop and her pencil case was placed on top of her notebook on the right of her laptop. She moved each piece around as if she were playing chess before finally sitting back and taking a sip of her coffee whilst waiting for her laptop to connect to the wi-fi.

Realising that she was being carefully observed she commented, "Work should be an art form, if nothing is in its place then it is a form of chaos. No one wants a chaotic agony aunt." She said this with a twinkle in her eye that showed how much she valued her work.

"Interesting," Dan replied, pulling out a notebook. "So once you are prepped, what do you do?"

"So, we start by logging into our emails and seeing how many we have." She stated this as she typed in her password into her *Proton* account and waited for them to load.

150! "Woah, that is a lot of emails." Dan exclaimed, confused by Jenna's nonchalant face.

"Yeah, that is normal. The most I have had in one day was 400! Now that was insane," she laughed. "Right, so next, we spend an hour reading through the emails and starring the most urgent ones. Now usually I would do it all on one laptop. But as I have a shadow…" She grinned at him, passing him another laptop from her bag. "You can look through some too! This is my spare one, it's a bit slow but I feel it matches its shadow well." A smile spread across her face. *How long did it take her to think of that joke?* he thought sarcastically.

"Oh hardy ha! OK, so what am I looking for? How do I know if it is urgent?"

"Good question, we will go through the first two together and you can tell me what you think."

Dear Jenna,

My cat has run riot around the house. It won't stay when I ask it to and it won't leave me alone. The other day I had to actually bath with it! I don't know what to do, he's ruining my life!

Help!!

From

Dave

Staffordshire

"What do you think?"

"I think he is nuts and needs help from a vet, not from you," Dan responded with a snort.

"Good answer, or get a dog. Much better behaved. Now I have responded to bizarre ones when they make me laugh but it is strictly for entertaining the readers. Obviously," Jenna replied. "Now you read the next one."

Dear Jenna,

I don't know what to do. I feel that my boyfriend is cheating on me. He is leaving at random hours of the night when I am asleep, he rarely talks to me anymore and don't even ask when we last had sex…

"Ahhh, erm…" Dan looked up, flushed as he was talking a bit too loudly which caused many of the older women in the café gasp in horror at the word. "Sorry!"

I don't know what to do or say. I love him and I can't bear the thought of him leaving me. What shall I do?

From

Sonia

Aylesbury.

"Oh, this one seems more pressing. Poor thing."

"Exactly, so we star it and go onto the next one."

This continued on for another hour: Jenna frantically reading and staring her emails from the bottom up; whilst Dan started from the top down. By the time they both got to Angela from Bristol, it was 9.05.

"Right, coffee and cake break before moving onto the writing! Same again?" Jenna pointed to the empty flat white mug next to Dan and he nodded in a daze.

"Yeah, ta." He continued to stare at the screen until the screen saver came on.

Up popped a picture of a woman who looked very much like Jenna, but this woman was happier. Her eyes sparkled in the camera and her smile covered her entire lower face. Her posture was of confidence and exaggeration. It took him a while to realise it was actually Jenna, but in a time where she was happy and young. Around her was a man who looked around the same age. He was also beaming and laughing at whatever prompted them to take the photo. They looked very much in love. *I wonder what happened to him,* he thought. *Maybe this was the cause of her demeanour change.* He was in such deep thought he hadn't realised Jenna had come to give him his coffee until he heard her gasp.

His eyes shot up to see a frozen Jenna staring at the picture. "I… I must have forgotten to turn the screensaver mode off the old laptop," she stuttered. "How silly of me, you'll have to get me to log you in now." She stumbled at the keys and quickly logged back in.

"I'm sorry, I didn't mean to stare." Dan mumbled so no one else heard. "If you don't mind me asking, who is he?"

"Who? Oh, the man in the picture? That's Liam. My… um… husband. He's gone." She looked in pain as she said the last two words.

"Oh, Jenna. I am so sorry." And there it was. The reason behind it all. The loss of a loved one, however close, must be horrendous. Not knowing any family apart from his gran, he could only imagine what it must feel. Empathy was not his strong suit but he tried to squeeze her hand in reassurance, but was not overly successful for she just yelped and spilled her coffee in her lap. "Oh, Christ, I am such a clutz. Sorry, Jenna."

"It's fine… honestly. Let's get on with the next step, OK?"

Chapter Eight

Shadowing Jenna Pace to Dan was like what David Attenborough does to wildlife. He was intrigued. He was hooked. He was surprised. What surprised him was the amount of effort she put into each letter: reading it twice, noting the main points in her note book, writing a draft letter before rewriting her letter a further three times then posting it on her blog. One more check and she was onto the next one.

Jenna had noticed that Dan had been silent for at least 45 minutes. He was like a toddler. First he asked a million why questions, then he kept walking off to get drinks or go to the loo, after that he would chat about random people on the street (that part Jenna didn't mind) and now he seemed to have exhausted himself and was watching Jenna's every move.

"You've been a this for two hours," he finally commented.

"How observant." Jenna smirked, not taking her eyes off the laptop. "It is lunch time now though so let's pause." And with a quick lock of her laptop, she jumped up and went to the queue.

"So, how do you get paid for this?" Dan asked.

"The website is subscription based," Jenna explained. "The money from it is split. It goes to me, to the blogging website company and it goes to my charity of choice. This year it is The Stroke Association. Last year it was NSPCC." Dan nodded in silence and chose his panini. He didn't want to pry into her choices of charity but a whole host of questions entered his head.

"Bacon and brie. Good choice." She smiled, also collecting a panini and a sausage sandwich. Before Dan could ask she stated that her friend would be there in a moment and that his favourite sandwich was a sausage sandwich, so she always got one for him.

As soon as she said this, Lionel burst through the door with a smile on his face. "Good morning all!" he shouted as he walked up to the counter. "Have you ordered my sandwich?" he asked Jenna, kissing her on the cheek.

"Have I ever missed a day?" Jenna raised an eyebrow.

"Well there was that one week…" he began before Jenna coughed at him.

"I was on holiday! In Greece!" she laughed as she passed the sandwiches to Perky Clarice who was smiling so wide it was sickening. "What has got you all hyped anyway?"

"Nothing, just happy the sun is finally shining!" He leant in and whispered, "And who is this charming man who is staring at me?"

"Oh, sorry. Lionel, meet Dan. Dan, Lionel. Lionel is my café buddy and sometimes helps me with my letters. Dan is my shadow." Jenna smiled.

"Nice to meet you, sir." Dan held out his hand.

Lionel paused. Looked at him up and down. Looked at Jenna then they both burst out laughing.

"Nice to meet you too, my boy. But Lionel will do. None of this Sir business if you please." Lionel stretched out his hand in response. "Now, let's eat and see who we have to save today!"

The rest of the day went pretty quickly. Lionel

gave a few of his own twists on the responses, which Jenna sometimes accepted and other times did not. They laughed and drank more coffee (sometimes tea). Before they knew it, it was closing time.

"Wow, I think I have completed a record amount of responses today, I might not have to do any tonight!" Jenna proudly stated as she turned her laptop off.

"You do this at home too?" questioned Dan.

"Of course, it's a full-time job, don't you know?"

"Well I do now!"

"Good," Jenna laughed. "Because you are taking the lead tomorrow. All responses from you. I will do a blog about a guest writer and you can continue it."

Dan froze in horror. "Me? Be an agony aunt?"

"Don't be stupid… an agony uncle," Lionel bellowed, glancing at his watch. "Oh, look at the time, best be off! Night, lovely lady. Night, sir." And off Lionel went.

"What a charming man," Dan chirped as they left Perky Clarice with tidying the café.

"He is indeed. So same time tomorrow? Or have you changed your mind and want to do the interview instead?" Dan still sensed the hopefulness in her voice.

"Nah. I am enjoying this too much. See you tomorrow, 8am!" he shouted as he walked to his car.

Jenna couldn't help but believe, as she watched him leave, that she wasn't going to get rid of him any time soon.

Chapter Nine

Helga was singing in the kitchen when Margot came home. She walked around the corner to see her dancing, by herself and whilst washing up, to *Just The Way You Look Tonight*, completely oblivious to Margot's presence. Margot had never seen her as happy as that moment. Washing up and dancing was something the twins had never seen her do before. Sure she danced with them as children and sometimes danced when hoovering but never when washing up. Just as Helga span around with a bowl she saw Margot staring at her and jumped, smashing the bowl in the process.

"Oh bother," moaned Helga looking down at the tiny fragments of bowl. "I'm sorry dear, I didn't see you."

"Sorry Gran, I should have warned you I was in.

I'll clean this up and you pop the kettle on."

"Good plan." And off Helga trotted to the kettle and began to fill it.

They just sat down with a cup of tea when Dan burst through the door.

"Ah nice one, any more for me?" he asked, twinkling his eyes at the thought of tea and biscuits.

"In the kettle," Margot and Helga snorted in unison.

Whilst Dan sulked off to make more tea, Helga sat smiling in her own little world. She had a few more hours before she had her dance class: Ballroom. This would be her second session and she loved it. Especially as she had company to go. Pottery class went awfully wrong so they tried dancing which was a hit.

"So, when are you off then?" Margot enquired, seemingly more interested in potentially stalking the couple to make sure they didn't go anywhere suspicious.

"In about an hour, dear," she replied with a smile.

"And where is the dance hall?" Dan chirped in from the kitchen. "Anywhere we know?"

"No dear, not anywhere you know. Anyway, how

was your week? I didn't get chance to ring you and see how you were."

"Ah, the usual. Work, work, work," Dan replied, rolling his eyes and miming typing. Truth was, Dan was having a great time. It was only one week in but he could really see how much Jenna made a difference in people's lives. He had written his own letters to others which had many positive responses and he loved it. For once, he got up for work without oversleeping, he worked to a respectable time and then he went to sleep and slept straight through. The Red Bull shares must have plummeted. "But, I think I should stay one more week. Just to be sure. Or maybe two. The article isn't due until next month so I have time."

"Eurgh," Margot moaned. Unknowingly at first she said it out loud. She glanced up and saw her gran and brother staring at her, confused. "It's just that… er… well Gran misses you and your room still isn't tidy and stuff."

Gran laughed and looked at Dan. "Well, apparently I miss you more than I realised." Glancing over towards a red-faced Margot, "I do miss you, dear, but I am also very proud of you. You must be doing great work there for you to want to continue. And for Jenna to keep you on. I bet she's so difficult to work for. Is she as perfection-esque as she seems?"

"Yeah, kind of," Dan lied. Yes, she had OCD with where her stuff went. But anyone would tell you it's just organisation in order to concentrate. She was funny and she really cared about the people who write. She wished she could help them all which hurt her when she couldn't. But difficult? No. She wasn't difficult at all. She was sweet, funny, kind, humble and very modest. Not the girl people thought she was, from her book. He sighed and smiled at his family. "She's alright, I guess."

"Well, I better head off. I'll be back later," Margot replied. "Nice to see you, bro. Gran, please don't do anything silly. Night all." Off Margot trotted out of the door and her headlights lit the living room as she went.

"I better get sorted too," Helga said, walking off leaving Dan alone. *I better tidy by myself then,* he thought whilst collecting the mugs up.

Now, Margot wasn't one to be annoyed but she was getting desperate. Later and later she had had to go to the hotel to stop fate from making her bump into her brother. She tried another hotel, but it was just too much. Why? Why was this happening to her? Was it because she was being dishonest? Because she hadn't told a soul about it? Or was it simply bad luck? Margot didn't know. All she knew was, she would be glad when things were back to normal so they could go back to normal times and the secret wouldn't be at risk of exposure.

Chapter Ten

It had been two weeks since she first met Dan and she could honestly say that she misjudged him. Dan had the sense of humour. Not due to being smug or cockiness, but out of loving life. His writing wasn't too bad for a temp journalist and she could see that he was a really hard worker.

As she sat watching him at the counter of the Roast Bean, she could see his smile just radiated the room. The women who walked in were instantly captivated by his manner and the older ladies giggled like sixteen-year-olds when he winked at them. But today seemed different. He appeared to be a bit more flirtatious than normal.

"Yeah," she saw him mouth to Perky Clarice, "I'll pick you up at 8pm. See you then," and he walked to the usual spot in the café. "Hey boss," he grinned.

"Hey Dan, everything OK? You seemed to be a long time with Clarice today." Subtlety was not Jenna's strong point.

"Er… yeah. Well she was saying about how her car broke down and that her band was playing at a pub just outside of town and she asked if I'd drive her then watch her show," Dan replied. He wasn't convinced that Clarice only wanted him for his car, but going and doing something other than writing his article at night seemed like a good idea. Besides, Jenna's reaction was too fun to ignore. "Why? Jealous?"

"Why… why would I be jealous? It's a band." Jenna rolled her eyes and turned her laptop on. "Right, let's get started."

A few hours went by and a few blogs from the pair had been posted. Lionel came in for his sandwich and coffee, but chose to sit at another table so as to not distract them.

"I'll only hold you back," he said with a weary smile. "I'm a bit tired today." This comment not only worried Jenna, but Dan as well. They both gave a silent look as if the one knew what the other was thinking and decided to keep an eye on him.

Dan was so busy typing that he almost missed it.

But luckily his peripheral vision worked like a dream. In the corner of his eye he saw Margot racing up the road. Well, he couldn't be sure it was Margot as it was raining and her hood was over her head but he was convinced it was her. She had the same walk and trot as Margot. It had to be. What was she doing here? He watched her out of the window and saw she walked into the Grand Hotel again. He wanted to stalk her but felt like she'd truly hate him for snooping.

"You OK, Dan?" Jenna questioned as she saw him stare into the distance.

"Huh? Yeah, it's just… Wow, look at the time. I better be off if I am going to get back here by eight. You mind?"

"No, no. Not at all. Have a lovely time." Dan didn't even notice her weak smile as he practically ran out of the door.

***

So he couldn't help himself. He snooped. Dan wandered into the Grand Hotel and looked around. He couldn't see anyone there but that wasn't to say Margot wasn't in the lobby.

He carefully walked around the corner to the concierge's desk. "Excuse me, um, Karen?" Dan looked at her name tag.

"Hi there. Welcome to the Grand Hotel. Do you have a booking reference?" Karen appeared to have the same sentence on repeat like some kind of state of the art AI system.

"Um. No. I was wondering whether a Margot Avery has checked in?"

"Margot Avery…" Karen's nails tapped the keyboard as she typed. "No. No Margot Avery. There is another Avery listed, however. A Dan Avery."

Dan was confused. Why would Margot be booking a room under his name? "Thanks Karen." Dan wandered out of the hotel and looked back into the lobby. No closer to working out what Margot was doing in a hotel like this.

***

Meanwhile, Jenna began packing up her things.

"I'm closing in five, Jenna. I have a date with Dan." Perky Clarice was almost smug as she looked at Jenna.

"A date? I thought it was a band rehearsal?" Jenna questioned, trying not to ask too pissed off.

"Oh, that was he thinks." Clarice's eye twinkled in

the dimming light of the café. "But it is actually a meal at the Rouge Lion. I am so excited, so please hurry. I need to get ready. Eee!"

Clarice's perkiness annoyed Jenna at the best of times. But smug Clarice was even worse. "Of course, let me get my laptop and I'll be out of your hair."

"Great. Have a lovely evening, Jenna," Clarice smirked.

"Yes, thanks. And you." Jenna could hardly breathe when she heard Clarice respond:

"Oh yes. I will."

***

Jenna felt that there was only one way to deal with her annoyance at Clarice: drink.

Now was it sad to drink alone? Yes? Was she truly alone? No. Because Abby was on Skype encouraging her.

"Come on, drink. Now tell me, it can't be that bad." Abby smiled down the camera. "You don't even like him."

"I know that," Jenna replied with a slight slur. Gone were the days she could drink a bottle of wine and still juggle. Now, one sniff of a chocolate liqueur and she had the wobbles. "But he is shadowing me. Why isn't he doing the work with me? I am just left to work on my blog alone."

"But you like being alone. That is why you moved in the first place. Remember?"

Jenna hated that Abby was the voice of reason. The wise owl that told her how it was. Abby would never let Jenna punish or blame herself but was also the first to say if Jenna messed up or was wrong. Having said that, Jenna thought to herself, isn't that what friends do?

"I know, I know. But it's been nice. Maybe I should employ a helper!" Jenna cried whilst pouring another large glass of blanc.

***

"Clarice, you said this was a band rehearsal." Dan was angry. After waiting on Clarice for over 20 minutes, driving for 30 and then realising it was just a way to get him to date her, angry was an understatement. He was furious.

"I'm sorry," Clarice pouted with a giggle. "I just thought we could go for food and I couldn't exactly ask you in front of Jenna, could I?"

Dan thought that was an odd comment to make.

"We are just friends, Clarice," he huffed.

"Oh, please don't be mad. It's just a meal." Clarice swayed in the doorway of the pub suggestively. Dan was rather hungry.

"Fine. But it won't be happening again." Dan power marched into the pub leaving Clarice to trot behind.

***

"I don't need him." Jenna was on her second bottle of wine which usually meant she had 20 minutes before the tears which then meant that Abby had 20 minutes to sort Jenna out before a meltdown. "I've lived on my own for three years since Liam. I have built my own company. I am good."

"Yes you are, girl," Abby chanted. "Yes you are."

"So why do I hate it that she's with him and I'm at home?" Abby could see the tears rise in Jenna's eyes. She had 60 seconds.

"Jenna, have you thought about bringing anyone to the Christening next week?"

"Shit, is it next week? I completely forgot." Win. Successfully distracted. "Not yet. Maybe I won't. I don't know anyone who would want to go with me." Her bottom lip began to wobble.

"It's a christening, Jenna. Not a wedding. You don't need a plus one, I was merely asking."

Jenna, distracted by her phone, ignored that comment. She'd had a picture message from Clarice. A picture of Dan sat at a table, clearly unaware this photo was being taken and a caption that read: *See? Told ya.*

"See. Told ya? SEE. TOLD YA!" Fury rose in Jenna's body like water leaking from an open dam. She hated being played. She hated not knowing. Worst of all: she hated that she was angry.

"Jenna. Calm. It is just a meal. It means nothing. Go to bed. Sleep the wine off and go into work with a calm head and just see what Dan says." Abby meant it this time. There was nothing in the world that would stop Jenna from worrying, but she could stop her from being angry.

"Of course, you are sooooo right." Jenna fell slightly to one side. "I shall sleep. Night-night, you lovely woman, you," and promptly passed out.

Chapter Eleven

Dan hated himself the next morning as he walked into the Roasted Bean half an hour late. It wasn't even as if he'd had a late night working or even spent with Clarice. The moment he had eaten he left the pub and got to the hotel and brooded over Margot. Could he give an 'I'm worried about my sister' excuse twice to the same person? He wasn't sure.

"Jenna I am so sorry."

Dan started but was interrupted by Jenna who grunted and said, "Don't. Shout. Head. Hurts."

"Late night?" He raised his eyebrow at her.

"Just a tad. Let's just do work, not talk."

Clarice was also not as perky as normal as she stormed down the café and practically threw the coffees at Jenna and Dan before storming off again.

Jenna couldn't help but smile. She'd seen Clarice that morning and asked how her date went:

"Urgh. He is so rude and obnoxious. You can have him," she stuffed at Jenna.

"What makes you think I want him?" Jenna shot back whilst massaging her temples.

"The way you look at each other. And he couldn't stop talking about you. Total bore." And she stormed off to serve a customer.

Dan saw Jenna smiling and couldn't help but feel uplifted. The night with Clarice was boring and she was rather self-centred. He found himself talking about Jenna an awful lot and he wasn't overly sure why that was the case. But he felt at home with Jenna, she didn't judge him. She was far from the person she was when she wrote her book. The loss of her husband must have knocked her down a few pegs.

"Seen Lionel today?" Jenna asked Clarice with a smile.

"He was out buying flowers this morning," Clarice responded and walked away.

Flowers. Lionel didn't strike her as a flowers kind of guy. She shrugged it off and went to work.

Dear Jenna,

My wife passed away a ten years ago and I have struggled to cope. We were married for years and I love her with all my heart. It pains me when I remember that she has gone.

However, I have recently met someone and I have found myself smiling again. I have never danced as much as I have danced since I hit 60. My laugh is back in full swing and I have found a skip in my step.

But I am worried. Am I cheating my wife if I am happy? Should I be mourning her forever? What shall I do?

From

An Old Man

Jenna put her hand on her chest and sighed. Should people mourn a loss of their loved one forever? Or should they move on and find new people to love? Some say there are soulmates out there. Jenna didn't want to believe that was true otherwise she was doomed for the rest of her life.

Dear Old Man,

First, I am so sorry for your loss. Grieving isn't easy and coping can be very hard indeed so I applaud you on your strength.

Second, I think there is a real merit here in wanting to have a skip in your step. I am convinced of one thing: for you to be mourning her for ten years must mean that you are an amazing man and that your wife must have been an amazing lady.

For that knowledge alone, I know that she would never ever have wanted you to be mourning for that long. Nor would she have wanted you to feel guilty or sad for finding someone who makes your heart skip a beat again. She would want you to live. So live your life and when, one day, when you see her again, you can tell her the adventures you have been on. She will be happy you have lived your life in her memory but also in your own.

I hope this helps you.

From,

Jenna

As she clicked 'send' she saw the date and remembered the conversation she had with Abby last night.

"Shit," she murmured.

"What's up?" Dan asked, popping his head out from the laptop.

"My godson is getting christened and I don't have a plus one."

"Christenings are places to take dates? They've changed since I've been to one." Dan smiled sarcastically and ducked as Jenna threw a napkin at him.

"I surrender!" Dan gasped, waving the remaining napkin. They both laughed until Clarice told them off for throwing things.

They stifled a giggle and carried on typing.

"I could go? You know, if you wanted to." Dan whispered so Clarice didn't glare at them again.

"You've got work to do, Dan. You have a least another hour," she teased.

"No. I meant to the christening. If you wanted to, that is."

"You'd be my plus one?" Jenna tilted her head to one side. "Why?"

"Helping out a friend. Besides, imagine Clarice's face when you tell her."

That was a reason Jenna couldn't say not to.

"Sure. Why not? It's Saturday. Is that OK?"

"Cool."

Silence ensued for the next few hours until Lionel came in.

"Lionel, how are you?"

"I'm great, my darling. Just great. I am just off to do some shopping. Going out to a restaurant tonight and want to look my best."

"Who's the lucky lady?" Dan asked.

"No one you know, young man," Lionel replied. "See you later, you two."

"He is the nicest man. I'd love my gran to meet someone like him." Dan smiled.

"He is the dream," agreed Jenna. "Now, get back to work," she smirked.

I have a plus one for the christening. Love you xxx

Who? Love you too xxx

… Dan….xxxx

WHAT?!?!? Tell me everything. xxx

It's nothing. Just he volunteered to come with so I wasn't on my own. xxx

Yeah… sure….xxx

Jenna couldn't help but snort. It was clear he only volunteered to annoy Clarice. There was nothing romantic or sexual in his volunteering. Was there?

Chapter Twelve

Helga had never been so excited. She was going out for a meal at the prestigious *Le Chateaux Orange* which had been the talk of the town since its opening in December. As she dressed for her date, she was going over and over the last few weeks.

Who would have thought that Helga, a widower, could find such a lovely man who would be willing to take her to all of these various locations and would stick by her whilst she dragged him to pottery class, real-life art and salsa dance lessons. *What a whirlwind*, Helga thought. She had mentioned the restaurant previously and hadn't thought anything of it but he was clearly listening. Helga sighed at her reflection and put her favourite earrings in.

"Whoa, Gran. You look stunning," Margot smiled,

peering into Helga's room. "Where are you off to tonight?"

Helga could hardly contain her excitement as she explained that her lovely man had booked a table at *Le Chateaux Orange* and how it usually gets booked up for months but he knew someone who knew someone else and now they were going.

"Wow, that is crazy. I've been there once but it took us ages to get a table." Margot froze as she finished her sentence.

"Who did you go with?" Helga asked.

Margot panicked, who could she have gone with? "Work. It was a work thing."

Seemingly convinced, Helga walked past Margot and started walking down the stairs, well, skipping down the stairs. Margot relaxed just before she heard a crash and a scream.

Helga, too excited for her date, had missed the last two steps of the stairs and was in a crumpled heap at the bottom.

"My ankle!" she screamed. "I've hurt my ankle."

Margot ran down the stairs to attend to her gran as the doorbell rang.

"That's him. Oh, this is a nightmare. Help me up."

Margot helped Helga to her feet and hobbled her to the front door.

"Well hello, my dear. Wow, you look stunning," was the response from the other side of the door.

A man in his 70s, peering over some bifocals, smiled at Margot and Helga. Margot shrewdly looked the man up and down, mentally taking notes.

He was slightly hunched, as most old men are, but he knew how to dress. He had a blue suit jacket with a purple pocket handkerchief. His tie was of the same purple material and his trousers looked clean and pressed to perfection. His shoes matched his outfit and you couldn't see his socks which shocked Margot. Usually older men had trousers that stopped at the ankle, showing holey socks. No, this man was sophisticated. This man knew how to dress. In fact, this man rocked the age of 70 very well indeed. Margot smiled at him approvingly.

"Oh my, what have you done Helga?" the man commented when he realised she was leaning off her leg.

"Hi, I'm Margot, Helga's granddaughter. Please, come in, I need to sit Gran down. She's had a fall and

I think she's twisted her ankle."

She ushered the man into their house as Helga just groaned. "We have a reservation, Margot. I need to get to the car."

"My dear," the man calmly sat next to Helga and stroked her hair, "we won't be going there. I will re-arrange for a few weeks' time." He paused. "Don't look at me like that, I will sort it. Margot, may I use your phone?"

Margot showed the man to the phone and got back to Helga. Upon looking at her ankle, she was concerned that it was a little more than a sprain. Bones at the Helga's age become more brittle and soft. Margot made the call to take her to the hospital to get it checked out; she would ring the hotel and Dan on the way.

As the man came back from phoning the hotel, Margot noticed he froze at a picture of her and Dan. Staring at the picture, he almost forgot where he was. With panic in his voice he told them that he had rearranged it for next month and asked if there was anything else they needed. Margot kindly told him that they were going to the hospital and not to worry, if he left his number she would contact him and keep him updated.

"Oh, thank you," he said before he turned to Helga. "Now, don't you worry. Just get some rest and hopefully it won't be long before you are up dancing again." He gave her a big hug just before helping her to the car and then began to walk to his own.

"Oh, I forgot to ask for your name!" Margot shouted to him as he got in his car.

"Lionel," he replied cautiously. "My name is Lionel."

Chapter Thirteen

The night couldn't pass quick enough. Lionel had been pacing the floor of his house for an hour before bedtime, thinking and thinking about what he saw that night.

The picture. The picture was burnt into Lionel's memory and he couldn't get it out. *Dan. Dan is Helga's grandson? Dan is the man that Helga is worried about working too hard? The man that is helping his dear friend and getting a story from.* He couldn't believe it. He just couldn't work out what he was going to do. He needed to speak to Jenna. What a dilemma.

He thought back to two days ago when he sent a letter to Jenna's blog about his wife. He loved her dearly. They met at 14 and were married at 16. She was the love of his life and always would be. But Helga. Helga numbed the pain of losing his wife.

Nothing could ever replace what he had with Evelyn but he needed someone. Someone to laugh with again. And when he finally found that, he panicked. Jenna's response was so lovely and heartfelt, he knew he was doing the right thing for him and Evelyn. In fact, he was going to tell Helga at the restaurant that he may be falling for her. But now? *Oh, bother,* Lionel thought.

***

8am came and Dan was sat with his coffee observing the road whilst Jenna set up her laptop.

"You know, you could turn yours on?" Jenna started at Dan. "You know, so you can type on it?"

"Huh? Sorry, yes. Switching it on means I can do my job, right?"

"Right!"

A few moments passed and Dan couldn't help but think about Margot. The worry had been mounting and now with Helga in a cast from falling down the stairs and breaking her ankle, he was even more anxious than before.

"Jenna, I was wondering if I could run an errand before doing this? I am really sorry but I can't concentrate until I have sorted it out. Is that OK?"

The stress in his voice made Jenna realise he wasn't just trying to avoid work. The sparkle in his eyes was dim and the wrinkles that were from smiling looked like they were from stress.

"Of course, take as much time as you need," Jenna responded, touching his hand and adding, "if you need anything, let me know."

They stared at each other for a moment. Forgetting that they were touching hands. The spark between them felt strong, or was it nervous? Neither of them could work it out. Jenna quickly retracted her hand and looked back at her laptop whilst Dan jumped up and went to sprint out of the door. At that moment, Lionel sheepishly walked through the door.

"Oh, sorry Lionel. Got to go."

Lionel just nodded and raised his hand in response before walking to Jenna.

"I need your help," was the only thing he could manage to say to Jenna, whose face went from happy to worried in less than 60 seconds.

Lionel explained the situation to Jenna. About responding to Helga in the first place, the dancing, the pottery, the letter to Jenna (who found it very flattering but also annoying that he didn't speak to her in person) and then the picture he found.

Jenna's mouth was wide open in shock. "So, you had no idea that Dan was Helga's grandson?"

"No, she never mentioned his name."

"So… you're dating Dan's grandmother?

"Yes. You know I've answered that question five times now. What am I going to do?"

Jenna paused for a moment. What would she do? *Poor Lionel*, she thought. *He is finally happy again and now this happens.* "The only thing you can do, Lionel, is to be honest with her and Dan. When he comes back you must take him to one side and tell him who you are. Dan has been worried sick that Helga has been going with someone unworthy. He loves seeing you and having you around. He may be perfectly OK with it!" She smiled, attempting to convince Lionel.

"And if he is not?" Lionel retorted.

"Then we deal with that bridge when we get to it. Now, how about a coffee?"

***

Dan sat in the hotel lobby for half an hour. He knew Margot would be there soon. He'd spoken with the lady on the front desk, gave a dazzling smile and got the day-to-day schedule of the visitor as well as the room number.

He stared at the door from above his newspaper. He realised instantly that he would never have been a good enough spy as he stood out like a sore thumb and had only watched comedy sleuthing programs. He decided he wouldn't apply to become the next James Bond either.

Suddenly, Margot walked quickly through the door and began to march up the stairs. Counting to 20, Dan began to follow. He knew the room number and so it wasn't about finding where she was going. It was finding who she was with. *I have to know*, Dan repeated in his head over and over.

201. 202. 203. 204. 204! He found it. His stomach was doing knots. His eyes narrowed and he felt sick. He slowly raised his hand and knocked the door.

"Coming," responded Margot's familiar voice.

As the door clicked open, Dan saw the colour drain from Margot's face.

"What… What are you doing here? How did you find me?" Margot stuttered, looking behind her in fright.

"I saw you. You were the reason Jenna wouldn't

interview me. I saw you here and I didn't know why. Gran has been worried sick about your whereabouts and I needed to know what you were doing. So what is it? Hmm? Why are you here?"

Dan stormed into the room before stopping dead in his tracks. Like a deer in headlights he stood, staring at a man and a woman sat at the table with a newspaper.

"Hello, Dan," croaked the man. "How lovely to see you again."

The woman next to him was weeping and couldn't make any words come out of her mouth. Dan stared at them in disbelief. He turned to Margot in horror and betrayal.

"After everything Gran has done for us. You're doing this?" He shook his head and began to leave.

"Wait!" The woman stood up, causing Dan to turn towards them. "Please don't leave us," she cried.

The man nodded and continued, "Please. Stay."

"Dan, please," Margot begged. "They are our parents."

Dan walked to Margot, his face inches away from hers as she silently wept.

"They are no parents of mine," and stormed out of the door and out of the hotel.

Chapter Fourteen

J enna had worked for seven hours and there was still no sign of Dan. She was wondering if he had sorted what he set out to do but felt it was not her place to get involved.

She checked her phone.

Nothing.

She checked her emails.

Also nothing.

Jenna sighed and shut down her laptop. Time to go home, put her feet up and open a bottle of wine.

Dan had been drinking since 1 o'clock in the afternoon and so by 7pm it was safe to say he was wasted. He walked for what felt like miles and miles pondering over his dilemma.

Why was Margot with their parents? What do they want? Why had they showed their faces after all this time? More importantly: why didn't they contact him? As he stumbled towards the Roasted Bean he realised that it was shutting. How long had he been out for? And he didn't contact Jenna to say he wouldn't be back.

"Well that is just great!" Dan shouted at his reflection in the window. "She's going to hate me. Well done, Daniel."

"Dan? Are you OK?" Clarice was stood at the door of the Roasted Bean about to lock up. "Do you need a lift anywhere?" For her faults and the fact she tricked him, Clarice did appear to be a nice enough person. He knew he couldn't keep walking and he wasn't 100% sure where his hotel was as everything was blurry. Where could he go?

"Yes. Yes, you could take me somewhere." He grinned as Clarice asked him where he wanted to go.

***

Jenna's wine bottle was nearing the end and Spotify was blasting out some epic tunes across the house. Lucky for Jenna, she was in a detached house and therefore her neighbours rarely heard her music playing. She was dancing around the living room when she heard a knock at the door. Praying it wasn't her neighbours, she was shocked to see a rather drunk Dan being propped up by Perky Clarice.

"I found him shouting at himself by the Roasted Bean, he said he needed to come here so here…" She passed Dan to Jenna before walking off. "You can have him," she finished.

Unsure what she meant, Jenna thanked her and offered her taxi money but felt very happy when she refused.

Dan dragged himself into her house and plonked himself on the sofa. "Oooh, wine," he commented, picking her glass off the table and downing it.

"I would offer you some but… well, you drank it," Jenna remarked with her eyebrow up in mock annoyance.

"It seems I have," Dan responded. "Have you got anything else?" He walked towards what he presumed was the kitchen and ended up walking into her downstairs loo.

"Well, there won't be any in there." She laughed before guiding him to the kitchen. Dan proceeded to choose his own bottle of wine and poured two glasses.

"Wanna hear about my life?" Dan questioned mid-sip.

"Go for it," Jenna replied.

Dan cried. Drank wine. Cried. And drank some more. He poured his heart out to Jenna which made her heart squeeze. She couldn't believe how sensitive he was. She found herself listening intently to every word he said and could only take sharp intakes of breath when he mentioned seeing his parents after 25 years.

"That must be so rough," Jenna finally said after downing the last part of her wine.

"Yep. I should write a book! The tragic tale of Dan Avery!" he shouted in response.

After opening another bottle of wine, he turned to Jenna and asked a question he'd wanted to ask since he met her. "So what's the deal with you?"

"Excuse me?" Jenna laughed at such a question.

"Like, what happened to you to make you change? I saw the interview for your book. You were savage. But now, you're lovely and sweet and gorgeous."

Blushing, a slightly drunk Jenna thanked Dan and shrugged her shoulders. "I lost my husband. It was a shock to the system. I couldn't be the person I was before because he made me that person. He kept me from being any different. He saved me from me. When he went, I just couldn't pretend I was confident. I ate to cope with my pain. I gained weight. I lost the part of me who held the, what did you call it? Savageness." She laughed. "It just wasn't me anymore."

Dan had stared intently at Jenna's face, observing her every change in expression. How had he not seen how gorgeous she was? How humble and kind she had been? Letting him into her life and her job must have taken so much courage. She was braver than even she realised. Before Dan knew what he was doing, he stroked the side of Jenna's face.

She froze, looking deep into his eyes, searching for some sort of response from him. He smiled, the smile that made her insides turn to jelly. The smile that made him more attractive than anything else.

"Sorry," he whispered.

"Don't be," she replied.

He leant towards her. "I just, feel like…" And before he even had time to finish his sentence his lips touched hers. The chemistry between them unleashed and the rest of the sentence was history. He wrapped his arms around her, as she did with him and they were lost. Lost in the embrace, the lust and also, the wine.

Chapter Fifteen

Dan woke up with a pounding headache. He rolled to face the sunshine and immediately regretted that decision. Squinting, he looked around the room. This wasn't the hotel room he as expecting to be in. *Where am I?* Dan questioned to himself.

Suddenly, something moved next to him and he was instantly transported back to last night. The wine, the dancing, the heartfelt conversation and that kiss. That kiss was nothing like he had ever experienced before. Just thinking about it gave him goosebumps and he so wanted to do it again. But would she? What did she think? Did she want him? He knew he asked way too many questions but he couldn't help himself. He found himself staring at her sleeping. His stomach interrupted his watching and he decided he'd go to make some breakfast.

As Dan crept out of the room, Jenna stirred. She beamed at the memory of last night. Never had she felt so safe, so happy. Happiness turned to worry when she saw the other side of her bed was empty and his clothes were gone. *Oh my god,* she panicked. *He's left, without a goodbye. Well done, Jenna. Messed that up.* Her thoughts were disturbed by a crashing downstairs.

Tiptoeing down the steps she could see Dan at her oven.

"Good morning," she whispered, pointing to her head to signify her head was hurting.

"Me too. Banging," Dan whispered back. "Eggs?"

"In the fridge. What we making?" She smiled.

"Pancakes?" Dan questioned.

"My favourite." She grinned.

***

A few hours later, Dan and Jenna walked into the Roasted Bean to see Lionel sat at their table with an older lady sipping coffee.

"Good morning Lionel," Dan began. "I am so sorry I barged past you yesterday, I was on a mission to see someone… Gran?" Dan stopped himself from completing his sentence and looked at Helga sat next to Lionel. "What are you doing here?" Dan questioned, tilting his head like puppies do when they are confused.

"Sit down, dear. We need to talk." Helga smiled politely. "Hello, Jenna dear. Take a seat too." Jenna obediently sat down and ordered a large latte. It was going to be a long day.

It was safe to say, that as conversations go, Jenna found that the best conversation she'd heard in a very long time. Dan nodded and absorbed everything. He even shook Lionel's hand. He was so happy for them he positively shone.

"Oh, Gran. I am so happy for you." Then his face turned dark, almost depressed. Like a switch had been turned off. "I… I have something to tell you too."

From the best conversation… to the worst. Jenna watched as the life drained from Helga's face. The pain that Helga was clearly withholding had just risen to the surface and was written across her old face.

"Take me to them, Dan. Now," she demanded and without even hesitating, he was up and helping Helga to her feet. Dan looked at Jenna with the same pain in his eyes as was there last night. Before it all happened and he looked like himself again. Truth was, they were both him. One side of him was the happy-go-lucky man just trying to make a living. The other was a man in pain from being abandoned by his parents all those years ago.

Chapter Sixteen

Margot had felt so bad she stayed on the sofa of her parents' room that night. She couldn't get Dan's devastated face out of her head. She knew she shouldn't have kept it from him but they told her not to tell him. They told her he wouldn't understand. That no one but Margot would understand. And now, her whole family could fall apart.

"That's OK, dear," her dad spat as he ate his steak. "Besides, you have us still. What more could you possibly want or need, eh?"

But was that what Margot wanted? She questioned it over and over again. By 9am she was exhausted just thinking about it and decided to go to see Dan. As she got to the door it knocked and her parents looked at her confused.

"Is he back?" his mum asked hopefully as Margot peeped through the viewer.

"Shit. It's Gran," Margot said.

"Wow," Helga said sarcastically. "Who'd have thought I could hear through a door? Now open up, Margot."

As Margot slowly opened the door Jenna attempted to walk away but Dan was too fast and grabbed her hand. "Don't leave. I need you," he whispered, tears caught in his throat.

"Of course," Jenna replied. "I'll stay with you." His smile was weak and he held his breath whilst entering the room, still holding onto Jenna's hand.

"Mummy!" shouted Daniella as she charged towards Helga. "Margot told me about your leg, are you OK?"

"Don't 'Mummy' me." Helga's stern voice was petrifying. *No wonder Dan wanted her to go with him,* Jenna thought. "What the hell are you doing here, what are you doing with my granddaughter and why have you not told me you are here?"

Daniella broke down into tears like she always did when Tony shouted at her. Helga used to always reprimand Tony for doing so but she totally understood why now. She was so hurt, so betrayed and the fact they managed to brainwash Margot into seeing them made her heart constrict.

"Well, Mummy," Daniella started with a sniff, "we got back just before New Year and… well… I'm sor—"

"It's my fault, Helga." Markas finally spoke after staring at Helga and the rest of the group. "I told her not to contact anyone until we knew what was happening. Daniella contacted the house without me knowing and by then it was too late, Margot knew and there was no going back from that. I am sorry." He also sniffed.

Helga looked at Markas and was confused. Markas was never one to apologise, nor was he one to take the blame for hurting people. She looked even deeper at his face. His skin was yellowing, his eyes were sunken and he looked so old. Older than his time. Helga sighed.

"How long?" she said.

"How long what?" Markas abruptly replied, trying to remain composed.

"Have you got?" She sat on the edge of the hotel bed. She saw Dan in her peripheral vision sink to the floor, holding Jenna's hand tight.

"A year. Maybe."

Margot sobbed as Daniella cried. "The doctors are unsure. That is why we are here, Mum. The doctors in London are doing the best they can. They have told us to stay near. We couldn't leave and we were so scared. We tried to talk to you but when we spoke to Margot, well, it all made sense. She drove us to the hospital and got us the hotel on long-term. She has been an angel." Daniella grabbed Margot's hand and squeezed it.

All of a sudden, an eruption of laugher came from the door. Dan, who had been sat on the floor at the time, looked up at them. Tears glistened his face as he stood up and walked towards his parents.

"I'm impressed," Dan started.

"Dan," Jenna interrupted.

"No, Jenna. Not now. I have to say this." He shot a look at Jenna which made her sit by Helga.

"I'm impressed with your skills of brainwashing. I do it as a writer. Force people into believing something, even when it isn't the whole truth. I am sorry that you are sick. I really am. I am sorry, that you are trying everything you can. But you left. You abandoned us. You left your own mother to look after two children whilst you went on to write your music and piss about with groupies. How did that go, by the way?"

"We played a few gigs across America," Markas croaked. "Then we wrote for other people. They became successes. But the business. The business is cruel. We drank, we took drugs, we did the things anyone in the business did. We were ashamed. We wanted to write but we couldn't. We are sorry, Dan." As he said the last sentence, Markas raised his hand towards Dan. "Forgive us?"

Dan looked at his dad in the face. Forgiveness is something his gran always brought him up to do. But it is a very difficult thing to do when put in that situation.

He shook Markas' hand. "I can't. I'm sorry."

Daniella screamed a sob from the other side of the room.

"For Christ's sake, Daniella, I'm not finished!" Dan shouted, shutting Daniella up in her sadness. "I can't forgive you for leaving us. I may forgive you someday. But not right now. What I will never, ever, be able to forgive you for is that one, you put Gran through so much strain and pressure. But also, that you didn't come back to all of us. As a family." And then hugged his mum and dad tightly.

Jenna watched the family with tears in her eyes. They were far from being a family unit but at least things were said and changes could be made. She watched Lionel, who was holding Helga tight, and realised how he had actually fallen so deeply in love with her. Then she looked at Dan. Could he love her like that? Could anyone after Liam? She didn't know. She decided to slip away quietly down the stairs to the lobby and go back to the Roasted Bean, after all she had left her stuff there.

"Jenna." She heard a voice behind her and saw Dan running after her.

He ran straight up to her face, grabbed her and kissed her with passion and need.

"I'll see you tomorrow for the christening? Text me the details?"

Shit, Jenna thought, *the christening.* "Sure Dan," she replied, still a bit stunned by the kiss.

"Good, I best get back up there… and Jenna. Thank you." He squeezed her once again and ran back up the stairs before she could reply.

Chapter Seventeen

Christenings are the weirdest of things for someone who doesn't really understand the idea.

"So, the baby has a bath?" Dan asked in the car.

Jenna snorted so hard, Lucozade almost shot out of her nose and onto Dan's dashboard. "No! His head gets a little wet, that's all. And a prayer is sent over him, I have to say an oath and some other stuff I am unaware of. Then there is a party."

"A party that he won't actually remember as he is less than a year old?"

"Exactly."

"Hmm, OK." Dan seemed unconvinced but very calm as he was driving them to London. He had spent most of the evening catching up with his parents and was more relaxed knowing his gran would be OK.

As they pulled up to the church, Jenna's heart tightened. She hadn't been this nervous in a long time. Well, since she said yes to Dan's shadowing idea. She walked into the church and instantly saw Abby. Her heart skipped a beat as she mock ran to her with her arms wide. She hugged the mum and dad, and most importantly Bobby, before introducing Dan to them.

"Nice to meet you," Abby started. "I have heard so much about you."

"None of it is true, I promise," Dan smiled.

"Wow… no, I believe it is." Abby smirked at Jenna. Jenna hadn't had chance to catch Abby up on their night together but Abby had an idea, especially as they were holding hands.

"We probably should sit right?" Jenna questioned Abby, pointing to some seats that said *reserved for Jenna and boyfriend*. She shot Abby a look of horror and Dan burst out laughing.

"Ouch," he cried, pretending to be wounded. "Me being called 'boyfriend' is so horrifying to you, is it?"

Jenna laughed it off and was glad he saw the funny side. "Abby can be a bit forceful when she wants to be, sorry."

"I like the sound of it to be honest." Dan grinned and kissed her forehead.

Jenna looked forward and ignored that comment. Too much going on today to think of that.

The christening went smoothly, until Bobby pooped on the vicar and then cried because the water was cold. The church lot began walking to the party when Dan pulled Jenna to one side.

"I'm not sure whether you heard what I said earlier?" Tilting his head again.

"I may have." Jenna looked at the floor and continued to walk forward.

"Now, I am not saying I want to rush into anything." Dan brushed his hair in his hands. "But, maybe I can take you out sometime?"

"I'd like that," Jenna smiled as they walked into the village hall as Abby ran towards her.

"Oh my god, Jenna I am so sorry. I let Jason send some invites to his friends and I had no idea this would happen."

Jenna was still smiling from her conversation with Dan; she wasn't really understanding Abby's point.

"Abs what do you mea—" She froze as she saw a tall, thin man in a pinstripe suit walk towards her. His hair was spiky and greying and his stride was of confidence. Confidence also boosted by the growth linked with him. A blonde-haired, blue-eyed bombshell of a girl was walking with him.

No. No this cannot be happening. Jenna begged the cosmos to just open the floor up. She felt sick. Out of everything she ever thought would happen today. This was not one of them.

"Hello, Jenna. You're looking… well." He smirked at his blonde woman. "Aren't you going to introduce me to your date? I must say, he is rather dapper. How on Earth did you find someone like this? Paying him, are we?"

"Erm… yes. I… I mean, no." Jenna was shaking. How would she introduce him?

"This is my date, Dan." She looked up at Dan. His eyes still twinkled when he looked at her, the expectant face. She couldn't look at him when she said: "Dan. This is Liam."

"Her husband," he emphasised as he shook Dan's hand. Jenna ran out of the hall, not bearing to see Liam's smirk.

Chapter Eighteen

By the time Dan had caught up with Jenna, the tears were streaming down her face and she was crumpled on the side of the road.

"Jenna!" he shouted after her. "Wait."

She turned to face him and saw his face for the first time since she said Liam's name. A mixture of anger and confusion was sitting on those smile wrinkles and she couldn't cope.

"What just happened?" he shouted at her. "How? How is that Liam? You said you lost him? You said he was gone? You know what that implies, Jenna?" He was so angry. It made her cry even more. "You better explain yourself. I can't believe you'd lie to me. I can't… I have to go."

"No. Please no. I didn't lie." She sobbed through

the tears. "I just didn't tell you everything." She walked to the nearest bench and sat down, signalling him to do the same. "I'll tell you everything. No detail left. Then you can make your decision about me."

***

Jenna always looked back at her first meeting with Liam as one of the happiest days of her life.

When he bumped her into a puddle his eyes laughed with his booming laugh and he couldn't help but pick her up. She was obviously cross but was not prepared to say no when he asked her for a drink. She went, fully entranced by his charm, and couldn't believe her luck.

After a few weeks, she was completely besotted by him, and him her. They went for meals. Went to the cinema. Walked for miles every night. As she was writing her book, he helped her by massaging her, making her tea and also making sure she was satisfied elsewhere.

Fast forward a year and they moved in together. He was just as dashing as always and she was getting ready to publish her first and only book. They were happy. Life was great and bliss.

Six months later she had a weird message from a

girl claiming to be Liam's girlfriend. At first, Jenna dismissed it. Then, after the fourth call, she confronted Liam about it. He explained it perfectly.

"I was with her, once. Just before I met you. I left her the moment I set eyes on you. I love you, mush." And kissed her. Everything was fine once he kissed her.

So she ignored the messages. The calls at 5am. The letters sent to her from this 'Lara' person. He would just laugh it off and kiss her. Everything was fine once he kissed her.

There was silence for another six months. Jenna was doing a book signing at her local Waterstones when Liam arrived to take her home. He was quiet and somewhat excited. She couldn't understand why. That was, until she walked through the door. Their flat in London was covered in her favourite roses. Candles (fake ones due to a fire risk) were scattered around the open lounge and the smell of her favourite meal, roast beef, was filling her nostrils.

As she walked around the room, fully embracing the romance, Liam bent down on one knee and proposed. She had said yes. She loved him with all her heart and they were married three weeks later.

Jenna noted that about two months into the marriage Liam had begun to change. Jenna's success was increasing as Liam's job was becoming more stressful. He was home later and later. He didn't want to hug her or sleep with her. She was worried. That was before the drinking started.

The first time it happened was six months after they were married. He had gone out with the lads, got pissed and Jenna was asleep on the sofa waiting for him as she had done so many times before. As he walked through the door, he tripped over her bag that was next to the door dropping his keys and smashing his kebab on the floor.

Jenna, being Jenna, ran to check he was OK to be greeted by a slap around the face.

"How many times have I told you to put your bag in your wardrobe?" he spat at her, picking up his kebab and walking into the spare room.

Jenna woke the next day to a big bouquet of flowers and an apology for getting mad but next time, put the bag in the wardrobe. He came in from work and kissed her. Everything was fine when he kissed her.

A week later she had gone out with a newly engaged Abby. She had drunk a bit too much, she knew this, but decided to walk home rather than ring Liam to get her. As she walked through the door, Liam was stood next to the phone talking to Abby.

"No, she's here. Hey baby. Thanks Abby." He hung up and walked towards her. "You were supposed to ring me."

"I thought you'd be asleep, baby." She put her arms around him. "I didn't want to disturb you."

As Jenna looked at Liam she saw something in his eyes that scared her. He pushed her off him and began to shout.

"You little bitch!" he shouted. "You worry me by not calling and then think that is OK. It is not OK." He hit her. When she dropped to the floor, he kicked her. Then he left her on the floor and went to bed.

"Honey." Liam brought her breakfast the next day. "Honey, I have your breakfast." She stared at him. Tears in her eyes.

"You hit me," she sniffed.

"You scared me," he replied.

"That is no reason to hit me, Liam."

"Shhh, baby. Do you not remember? You put your arms around my neck when I was talking to you. I was only defending myself from drunken you. Really it should be you apologising to me."

"What?" Jenna was confused. He sounded so convincing.

"I forgive you, baby. Now, have some rest and I'll sort dinner out for tonight, OK?" And then he kissed her. Everything was fine when he kissed her.

One night, Jenna was making dinner when the phone rang. It was Abby. She got chatting and completely forgot about the dinner in the oven. When Liam came home, he saw smoke coming out of the oven and immediately saw red. Abby heard the anger coming out of Liam's mouth and was worried for Jenna. Jenna dropped the phone without switching it off as he forced her to take the food out of the oven without gloves. Abby could hear her screams from the other room and instantly called the police.

Liam was taken into custody but needed Jenna to press charges for it to stick. She loved him. She could help him. He needed help, not a cell. She came up with an excuse at the hospital, explaining that she wasn't thinking straight due to the smoke alarm going off. He was released and when he got home, he kissed her. But everything wasn't that fine when he kissed her anymore.

He began to demand sex. He began to demand food. Demand cleaning. Demand she dressed in a certain way.

The final straw came on the day she found out she was pregnant. They were in the car driving back from his parents' house when she told him. She was so excited. He wasn't.

"What the fuck?" He raised his voice at her.

"What do you mean? I'm pregnant. We had sex. I'm pregnant." She was confused. Didn't he want this too?

"Great. Just great. I can't be a dad. I'm not ready to be a dad." Jenna could hear the anger rise in his voice. "For Christ's sake how could you be so stupid? We will book an appointment and you can get rid of it."

"Excuse me?" she responded in a loud tone. "I am not."

"Sweetheart. I need to be honest with you." His tone of voice changed very quickly. "I'm having an affair."

Jenna's world crumbled in half. Everything she had done for him. Gone. What was going to happen now? She couldn't be a single mother.

"We can make this work, Liam. You can leave her and we can start again."

"Listen, you stupid bitch," Liam responded. "Lara won't have me if she thinks you are pregnant. You can't be pregnant. Got it?"

Lara. Jenna had pushed that name to the back of her head years ago. She saw red. How could she be so blind? She shouted at him. Swore at him and he just sat there. Until she threatened to leave him.

"Oh no. You are not leaving me. That is not an option." And with that he tried to grab the wheel. "If you leave me, I will kill you. Got it?" And the last thing Jenna saw was the car coming towards them as their veered to the wrong side of the road.

When Jenna woke, she was disoriented.

"Mrs Ashton… Mrs Ashton… Can you hear me?"

"What? What happened? Where am I?"

"You are in the Royal London Hospital. You've had… you've had an accident. Do you not remember?"

"No, I was driving and then… oh God! Where's Liam? Liam! LIAM!"

Liam appeared around the corner with flowers.

"Baby, you're awake." He kissed her on the forehead and sat by her side. He stroked her hair and turned to the nurse. "Thank you for helping my baby."

"Baby?" Jenna asked. "My baby is it…" She saw the nurse's face and realised what had happened.

Liam was a very good actor and began to cry. "We lost our baby. Oh, if you only hadn't fallen asleep at the wheel."

Jenna froze. "That is not what happened, Liam."

"Well of course it was. What else would it have been?" He kissed her. Everything was never fine when he kissed her again.

She wrote him a letter explaining how she wanted to help him but she couldn't. That she was sorry but she had to go. He came to see her at the hospital. Begged her to stay and that he was sorry but she was done. She left the hospital and left for good. Finding solace in her South Norwood. Trying to mend her life.

***

Dan sat on the bench, exhausted from what he heard. Every emotion he felt during Jenna's life and all he wanted to do was hold her and tell her it would be OK. But instead he held her hand in silence. As he did, he felt his phone vibrate. It was Sheila.

"Hi, Dan darling, it's Sheila. The article has been pushed forward. We need you back to work and your article next week." Then she hung up.

"I'm sorry, Jenna. I have to go back home. The article has been pushed forward and I need to finish it." He gave her such a big squeeze she yelped. "Let me drive you home."

Jenna couldn't help being stressed about his lack of response. Could it be that he was using the article as an excuse to leave her forever? She couldn't bear to hear the answer so she just nodded and got in the car. Not even seeing Liam watching them from the window.

"Everything OK babe?" the blonde woman squeaked then flinched.

"Oh shut up, Lara," he replied, watching the love of his life drive off with another man.

Chapter Nineteen

Dan got into his work at record speed on Monday. His head was still spinning from Jenna's revelations and he couldn't quite understand how someone could hurt someone they love. Then he thought about his own family and realised people do it all the time. It's just not always visible.

Sheila was pacing the floor, as she often did when she was nervous, annoyed or generally feeling any emotion. If Dan had been doing his job, he would have had the article completed by now but no. He was at a christening of some friend of a woman who Sheila thought looked familiar. What was that about? She paced quicker. *He better have a story*, she thought to herself. She glanced out of the window. *Finally*.

"Where have you been?" Sheila began crossly. "I

thought you'd be in half an hour ago."

"I'm sorry Sheila, Gran needed help." Dan fluttered his eyelashes and once again she was calm. *How does he do that?*

"Yes, yes. Well sit down and tell me what you have."

"I've just walked through the door. Give me an hour and you'll have something, I just have to finish it."

Dan got up and left Sheila dumbfounded. He was never that confident before he left. She looked back at the pictures on Facebook. He looked so happy, so calm. Nothing at all like he did when he was at work. Very well rested. He looked back at the dark-haired woman holding the baby. She looked awfully familiar.

Then it hit her. Jenna! Sheila gasped. How could that woman be Jenna Pace? Sheila had always had a slim figure. One of those people who hated any form of fat and who had the strictest of diets. She never understood how people could just let themselves go. No understanding of loss, pain, anxiety as she had always been selfish and narcissistic. Sheila revelled in the picture whilst catching her reflection in the window.

Sheila continued to stare at the picture in disbelief. The confident bombshell of a woman Sheila had admired and followed like a saint. No. Sheila couldn't believe her eyes. She nodded. Jenna was a traitor to the cause of women; how could she lose what she had? She watched the interview over a dozen times; the woman in the christening picture was not Jenna Pace.

That was a woman who had lost her femininity and become a regular, boring person. *Shame,* Sheila smiled. *Looks like we all fall down from our pedestal eventually.*

Chapter Twenty

Dan was busy typing. He began his article the day he met Jenna and now it was coming to an end he felt... he didn't know what he felt. He hadn't rung Jenna since he got home. Nor was his plan to. It was clear she needed time to think, she was distraught after all. So he did what he always did and decided to put his energy into his work.

Finished. Work experience with Jenna Pace.

He read the article over and over again. Something did not feel right. The comparison of her first work with her agony aunt stuff. The comparison of her thinner lifestyle to the new fuller-figure her. No. He couldn't keep this article. He needed to write a new one. One that would show the true Jenna Pace. The woman who loved her life in South Norwood; who loved her friends; who always put her family first. More importantly, the woman he was falling in love with. The realisation hit him like a freight train. He loved her. The woman who barged into him that day and gave him all those one-word answers. The woman who let him into her life knowing her own traumas but still smiling.

She gave him life. She gave him something to wake up for that wasn't coffee and a cheap article for a crappy magazine. It was worth more than his job all over. He needed to see her. He needed to tell her everything.

As he clicked delete he ran out of the door, completely ignoring the box double checking to be sure he wanted to delete the article.

A few hours later, Sheila walked into the intern's office. She had a voicemail from Dan telling her that the article would be completed by the morning but he needed to be away from the office to complete it. She sat in his chair and sighed. As she glanced up she looked at the screen. He hadn't even logged off. As she woke the computer back up she noticed an article created by him.

As she read it, her eyes lit up. This would give her all the leverage she needed to be promoted. This article was the best article she had read in a very long time. Money symbols shone in her eyes as she sent the article to publishing.

Jenna would be ousted for being a fraud, but Sheila Renaulds would be a star publisher.

Chapter Twenty-One

Sitting in the Roasted Bean sat a natural-faced (and frizzy-haired) Jenna with her fifth cup of coffee. It had been three days since she had seen Liam and since then, she hadn't been able to function. Her website was offline whilst she dealt with her own damage control and it was all she could do to get up and out of the house each morning.

"If it wasn't for you, Lionel, I'd still be in bed." Jenna smiled painfully at her old friend.

Lionel chuckled and simply said, "It wasn't just my idea. Clarice and Helga wanted you to know they are on your side too. In fact, Helga will be here soon to talk to you about something."

Conversation with people, especially Dan's gran,

was not something she was overly enthusiastic about. But she would do anything for Lionel and she knew Helga would only want the best for her.

As for Dan. He got back to work on Monday and she hadn't heard from him since. *Probably wants nothing to do with me*, she texted Abby. *Don't blame him either.*

Don't be stupid, Jenna, Abby responded. *You had every reason to keep Liam's nature at bay. You were protecting yourself. He'll see that.*

And if he doesn't? Jenna asked, petrified of the answer.

Then sod him. x was her answer.

Jenna couldn't help but smile. Abby would never change and she certainly never wanted her to. She was the voice of reason she needed and although Abby blamed herself for what happened at the christening, Jenna couldn't be mad at her best friend.

"Jason slept on the sofa," Abby said when Jenna spoke to her the day after the christening. "Truth was, he didn't remember inviting Liam. He only invited Harry but Harry must have mentioned it to Liam."

"It's fine, Abby. Let's just forget and move on. I need to."

And they had. Back to how it was, but Jenna

hadn't moved on internally. She was a mess and needed help.

Helga stepped into the Roasted Bean with a notepad and pen. She kissed Lionel on the head and signalled to Clarise that she'd love a cup of tea.

"Jenna, dear. How are you?" she began.

"I've been better," Jenna replied whilst downing her last bit of her latte. "What is the notebook for?"

"Oh, I am so glad you asked. I want you to read it." Helga passed the notebook to Jenna and she opened it to the first page.

Her eyes widened as she realised what this was.

"I remember this letter. Lionel and I discussed what to do and how to respond." She showed Lionel briefly before reading it again. "Wow. Small world."

"Yes. Yes it is, dear. But what you haven't realised is that without you, I would not be here. I would not have met Lionel. I would not have understood why Margot was running around at night. I also would not have read your amazing book and I would not have seen Dan become the man he has become without you. So I have got some advice for you. Ready?" Jenna nodded in response, frozen in the words. "You are an amazing woman, Jenna. You are a strong woman who got through one of the worst moments anyone could ever think of. You're a survivor. Your husband never deserved your love. Just like you don't deserve to feel like this. You must continue your work. You must forgive yourself and you must love yourself again. Chapter 7: loving yourself again."

Jenna grinned at Helga. "You're using my own book against me. Low blow, Helga." She concluded with a laugh and then said, "Thank you."

At that moment, her phone rang. The screen said Dan.

"Hello?"

"Jenna. It's me. Dan. I was wondering if it was possible for me to come over later? Maybe around seven?"

"Sure, I'll be at home. See you then." And she hung up and turned to the old couple. "I better get back and tidy, Dan is coming over. I think this is a good moment to forgive myself and talk to him."

"Ah, young love." Lionel smiled at Helga. "Isn't it blossoming?"

"I think so, Lionel dear. I think so."

Jenna could only not react to this fact. She felt butterflies in her stomach but not because she was nervous and didn't want to see him. But because she couldn't wait to see him, hold him and tell him she loved him.

Chapter Twenty-Two

Within a few hours, Jenna had cleaned the house from top to bottom. She set candles around the room and sprayed perfume around the house. She was cooking spaghetti Bolognese when the doorbell rang.

5.15pm? He was mega early. She smoothed out her dress and opened the door.

"I didn't expect you to be here so soo—" She stopped when she saw in her doorway, was Liam. Not the suave Liam. But a tearstained, crushed-looking Liam.

"Hi," was all he could say whilst staring at her face.

"What are you doing here, Liam? How did you find me?" She couldn't breathe. He always said he'd find her. He always said if she left him, he'd kill her. Was this it? Had he tracked her down for this? Her chest was constricting as she tried to remain tall. "What are you doing here?" she repeated.

"I asked a few people where you lived. The townsfolk are very friendly." He smiled weakly at her. "I've come to see you. To apologise for... for..." He broke down there and then on her doorstep. He looked like the shell of a man to what he was at the christening or even during their marriage. Jenna knew she should just shut the door but she couldn't. Regardless of what had happened she was still a compassionate person and leaving him on the doorstep would be cruel.

"Come inside, Liam. Before the neighbours see you snotting my doorstep," she responded more abruptly than she meant to.

***

Dan was parked on the other side of the road, he was so early due to the excitement of seeing Jenna again. But he couldn't believe what he was seeing.

Jenna was stood on the doorstep but she was not alone. Liam was with her. *What does he want?* he growled to himself. The dilemma of the situation was, did he intervene or was that not his place yet? He couldn't work it out.

Then, Liam went to hug her. Jenna let him. *What?* He then kissed Jenna on the cheek then walked to his own car. She waved to him as he drove off then walked back into the house.

Just in view of the door, Dan saw candles in the room. Had they just had a date? Were they back together?

Rage was filling Dan's body. He gripped the steering wheel tight. How could she possibly have a date with him just before he was coming round? One thing was certain, Dan wasn't going to stick around to find out. He sped off back home, heartbroken, and decided to never think about Jenna again.

***

Jenna's phone beeped at 6.55pm.

Sorry. Can't make it tonight. Something has come up. Good luck with everything.

Dan

Jenna looked confused. Why would he cancel? Devastated, she glanced at the spaghetti Bolognese on the table.

"Looks like I'm having leftovers for a while," she said out loud, wiping a lone tear off her face.

Chapter Twenty-Three

Jenna was nervous. Today was the release of the magazine Dan worked for. All of her hard work had come down to this day; how would the article paint her? After the last few weeks, she wasn't sure. She tried contacting him but it kept going to voicemail and he wouldn't return any of her texts.

Whilst in line at the post office, she thought back to the last text he sent her. *Something has come up.* What was it? Was it his parents? Although, Helga hadn't mentioned anything recently.

Helga was just as baffled as Jenna was. "I just don't get it," she huffed, in the line with her. "He just said something had happened and he couldn't go back to South Norwood. Then he said that he hopes you're happy."

"Hopes I am happy? What does that even mean? Oh Helga, I just don't get it either. It just didn't sound like him."

"No. It doesn't. So have you heard from Liam recently?"

"He's in therapy at the moment so no one can really contact him. But from what I hear, he is doing great and signed the papers. By next month I will be divorced and I cannot wait." Jenna was so happy.

***

When Liam turned up on her doorstep she was petrified he'd hurt her. Turns out he wanted to apologise for his behaviour and explain how he was turning himself into a kind of rehabilitation centre where they discuss and address abusive behaviour.

"I saw your face when you saw me at the christening," he sniffed in her living room that evening. "I couldn't breathe, you looked so scared. Then when I saw you run away and that man was with you. It hurt. Oh, Jenna. It hurt me so much to see what I had done to you. I can't bear it. I couldn't believe I was watching you with another man. I couldn't cope." He paused and sighed. "I drank so much that night. It was such a blur. I woke up in hospital. Lara had, well Lara had left me because she saw my love for you and well, I had lost you and her in one day. I mean, I know I lost you ages ago but it hit me, you know? That I had really lost you."

Jenna was attempting to process the information, but was struggling to contemplate how he only felt this bad now. "Why were you in hospital?"

"I punched my hand through a glass window." He raised his bandaged hand up to her. "As Lara went to leave. There was blood everywhere. She was screaming and then all I remember is it going black."

There was a moment of awkward silence in the room.

"I can't forgive you, Liam. We lost our baby because of you."

A loud sob erupted from Liam. "I know. I think about that moment every day."

"It would have been three this year. Three, Liam. I loved you. I stood by you. I wanted to help you. But, I'd have died trying."

Another silence rang out in the room.

Jenna braced herself and said, "I want a divorce, Liam. I need to be free."

Liam nodded and ran his hands through his hair.

"I know. I need to let you go. I know I need help. I know I held on to you for so long, I owned you for so long. That was wrong of me. I need, I need to let you go. You deserve to be happy."

He looked around the room at all the candles. "Waiting for someone?" he smiled.

"No, I just like filling the room with candles for my own amusement," she grinned.

"Ha! I always loved that humour of yours." He stood up and walked towards the door. "I've kept enough of your time already. Goodbye, Jenna." He gave her a hug and kissed her cheek before walking to the car.

She was free. Jenna felt like a house had been lifted off her shoulders. She had never felt so empowered as she did that day. Only to be crushed back down to earth by Dan's text.

***

"Can I help you, miss?" the cashier said, jolting Jenna out of her memory.

"Oh yes, sorry. I've ordered a magazine. Jenna Pace."

"Yes, here you go," smirked the cashier. "A real read it is too."

Helga and Jenna looked at each other as they stepped out of the line and opened the page to Dan's article.

Work Experience with Jenna Pace

By Dan Avery

No one has ever been able to interview Jenna Pace, until me. I was lucky enough to not only meet her, but to get to know how she works. From writing her best seller 'how to save you from you', Jenna has fallen from grace into a spiral of hiding behind her laptop in order to fuel her need to help people...

"What?" Helga couldn't believe her eyes. She looked at Jenna, tears flowing as she continued to read it.

"Well, that is all you need to know about how Dan feels then," Jenna said, running out of the post office, hugging the magazine and leaving Helga calling after her.

Chapter Twenty-Four

Dan sat in his room, blaring tunes out of his laptop when he got the email.

Subject: You are a hit

He clicked on the email.

Dear Dan,

Your article on Jenna Pace was so successful. It was so heartwarming to see how nice you were about how much of a fraud she was. I don't think I could write something so nice.

Anyway, I want you to know you have been accepted to work full time at the magazine and we look forward to you starting right away.

Regards,

Sheila

Dan clicked the link and instead of his new article he'd sent the publishers, he old one had appeared.

"No, no, no!" he shouted.

Running to his phone he dialled Jenna. "Pick up, pick up."

"What?" croaked down the phone. "Ringing to gloat, are we?" She had obviously been crying, and possibly drinking. Dan felt terrible.

"Jenna. It's not what you think. That isn't the article I sen—"

"Save it, Dan. I can see what I was now. Just trying to make a name for yourself. Well, I hope you are happy. You've trashed my name just to make yours stand out. I can't believe I thought I was falling for you. Oh, there's another article forming. *Jenna Pace: fool and all around loser.* Goodbye, Dan."

She hung up and Dan was left staring at his phone. He understood why she was acting this way. He would too if someone implied he was a traitor to the self-help profession. But what could he do to fix it? How did this get published? And more importantly, she was falling for him?

***

Jenna had been in bed for what felt like hours but had actually been days. Her room was full of ice cream tubs, grape boxes (tried to be balanced) and empty wine bottles. Tissue balls littered the dark floor like stars in the sky and her hair was more bed than head. She read the article again for what felt like the one hundredth time. How could someone be so cruel?

Buzzing on her windowsill signified that Abby was ringing. Again. The fifth time this hour. Jenna rejected it once more. She couldn't bear to speak to anyone. She wasn't even able to talk to Lionel when he dropped off more wine. No. Abby would just have to leave her alone.

Opening her laptop, she saw she had 450 unread emails. *New record*, she thought. *Dan would have pretended to be impressed.* She couldn't believe what a fool she had been, trusting someone and letting them into her work and life. She vowed never to be interviewed again and just get back to her work.

Subject: I'm having an affair and want to let my husband know. How?

Really?

Subject: my girlfriend is allergic to dogs. Do I get rid of her or the dog?

Wow!

Subject: we believe in you.

Jenna stared at the email. *Hmm. What is this then?*

Dear Jenna,

We have read the article. I say we. We are the Saving You From You Club. We read your email responses and talk about your book. We try to help people in our local area and have set up our own newspaper article about it.

Anyway, we feel that you have been misrepresented. You have helped us all without even realising it. You have been the backbone to our society in ways you can only dream. Josephine, our editor, emailed you two years ago. Your response helped her to move out of her husband's house and into the freedom she deserved. She now has her own house and is with a lovely man who treats her nice.

Poppy, our feminist columnist, was helped by your book. She raves about being safe and happy with herself. She wasn't before. She was so shy and nervous.

Since seeing your pictures in that article we realise that although you are our hero: you are a person too. You deserve all the happiness you could ever want.

Lots of Love,

SYFY Club

Jenna sat in shock. People still believed in her. Over 50 emails were dedicated to the article, slamming its contents and declaring that they were on Jenna's side. All this time, she expected to be ousted from her love of helping others when actually it had helped them more?

She started favouriting emails. *Back to it*, she thought to herself as she picked up her hairbrush.

Chapter Twenty-Five

Margot arrived at the Roast Bean every day from 7am and left at 1pm in the hope of finding Jenna.

It was on day four that she finally found her.

"Jenna!" she shouted across the room.

Jenna looked up stunned. "Margot? What are you doing here?" She got up and gave her a hug. "How are your parents?"

Margot shrugged. "Same old, really. We are waiting for a liver transplant for Dad but it's more a matter of time than anything else. Can I sit with you? We need to talk."

For the next two hours, Margot had talked Jenna's ear off about how miserable Dan was. Jenna, at first, dismissed his feelings towards the article but by the end she had become more inclined to believe Margot's story.

"So you are telling me he didn't know?"

"Yes. I saw the article he was going to send. Or the article he thought he did send. Oh Jenna, he never would have wanted to hurt you. Not with your past and all." Jenna raised her eyebrow. "Oh shoot. Sorry. He had told me. He came back from the christening so stunned he couldn't not."

"It's fine. Honestly, Margot. But he still wrote the first article. He still thought that about me at some point to write it. I can't believe how stupid I am."

Margot sat and held Jenna's hand.

"You have changed our lives more than you know. First of all: Gran and Lionel. You know Lionel asked me if he could ask Gran out on proper dates? Yeah, he has really taken a shine to Gran."

Jenna smiled. Lionel did say he wanted to talk to Jenna about something, but she just palmed him off. She made a mental note to go round to his and apologise.

"Two." Margot hadn't noticed Jenna zone out. "Me and my parents. I didn't have the confidence to discuss it with anyone. But when we all talked at the hotel, it was you giving me the space to do so. And three: Dan. Oh, Jenna. He has always been obnoxious and arrogant. But he was so career driven he couldn't see it was killing him. With you, he took that step back. He made himself slow down and it was worth it. He found you. You made him the Dan I love. But never, ever, tell him I said that." She giggled like a schoolgirl. "I'd deny it, see."

It was Jenna who Dan wanted with him when he met his parents again. And it was him who invited himself to the christening. It was also him who asked her out on dates.

"But then why did he cancel seeing me? If he feels so strongly," Jenna objected. "Explain that."

"That? He saw you with Liam. Said he knew that he couldn't compete with someone you were married to. Love will always find a way and the christening gave you and Liam a chance to reconnect. He saw Liam leave and mentioned something about candles."

Jenna's face drained of colour. He saw Liam leave and presumed she was going to get back with him. So many questions floated around her head she could barely make sense of it all.

"I was ending everything," Jenna murmured. "I

asked him for a divorce. The candles were for Dan." She began to weep. Margot hugged her tightly.

"We will sort this out. I promise." She wiped Jenna's tears with a tissue.

Jenna's smile must have been unconvincing but Margot didn't let on. Because how could it be OK, when she turned to the love of her life and told him to never contact her again? She pondered over it whilst Margot went to get another coffee. She needed a plan and Margot would have to help her.

This would be the letter to end all letters.

Chapter Twenty-Six

an slumped into his new office. It should be a happy occasion with lots of celebrating. But if he was honest with himself he felt awful getting the full-time position. It wasn't fair to have hurt someone to get a job. In fact, it wasn't even the article he wanted her to see. It just didn't seem fair to him. So he couldn't be happy. He couldn't even be slightly thrilled. He felt miserable.

"Here he is! The big cheese!" Sheila shouted across the office block to his. "How does it feel to be in the big chair?"

Dan waved as if to say, 'Oh, stop it,' but she could tell he was annoyed about something.

"What's wrong, pet?" Sheila said. Her eyes were sparkling in her older age and her wrinkles had set into a grin position. "Not happy?"

"Meh." Dan could only manage a few noises.

Sheila was confused. This was what he wanted. Even the New York office called to congratulate so what was his problem?

"Come on, deary, be happy. This is all you have worked for! Let's make a toast." She lifted up her coffee mug. "To *Work Experience with Jenna Pace*. Oh, it was a brutal piece. Thank God I found it before it was gone forever."

Dan began to lift his mug then placed it back on the coaster.

"Excuse me? What do you mean before it was gone forever?"

Sheila looked terrified. Her pale face suddenly became bright red and her eyes began to search for an escape. Dan knew instantly that she was responsible for this.

"You sent that article? I thought I'd deleted it. But you, you sent it to the publishers? Why? Why wasn't my other one good enough? Why did you have to destroy Jenna's life?"

"Because that is business, Dan," Sheila spat. "The other one you wrote was cute at best. But it would never get you a journalist position at any firm. It would barely get you a website blog. But the one I sent, that was pure. It was so cutting that it has made you famous in our firm. Think about it, Dan. In a few years you could be running this place whilst I am with the big leagues in New York!"

"I've damaged someone I care about so I could be like you? Oh no. Not me. I can't even believe you could do such a thing. Not even for business. I'm out, Sheila."

"What?"

"You heard me. I quit." Dan stormed out of the office with Sheila shouting obscenities after him.

Chapter Twenty-Seven

"**C**ome on. Pick up." Dan was cursing down the phone in the hope Jenna would pick up.

Sorry. I am unavailable at the moment. Please leave a message after the tone.

"Urgh!" Dan yelled out of the window of his car. *Why does no one answer their phone nowadays?*

Dan had been driving for what felt like days but it had only been a few minutes. He was so nervous to see Jenna he could barely see the road.

How could Sheila do such a thing? He knew he needed to make it right. He didn't know how to though. What would make her see how much he meant to her?

Suddenly, it hit him. The only way he knew how to

make it right. He pressed dial again.

"Hi. Abby? It's Dan. Yes, I know it's horrible. I didn't mean to— will you just listen to me! There was a mistake and I need to fix it. So help me… Thank you."

***

Jenna was busy typing when Lionel and Helga walked into the Roasted Bean.

"Can't. Talk. Must. Type," Jenna stuttered over her seventh coffee.

"Oh." Helga smiled. "We best not disturb you."

As Helga and Lionel went off to another table, ordering a cappuccino as they went, Jenna waved them off. She had to finish her plan. Margot had helped her write some but she had to go for her Dad's appointment so Jenna was left by herself.

Just as she'd finished her first draft, she looked up and saw Abby in the door.

"Abs… what are you—"

Jenna was cut off by Abby who said, "Just listen." Her tone proved to Jenna that she was not in the mood for pleasantries. "For years, I have watched you disintegrate into a shell of what you used to be. You practically became scared of your own shadow. But with him, with him you became a better person. You became you again. Someone I have missed so much. I know what he has written, I've seen the true article. You need to read this, I have emailed you. Then go to the place you first met."

Jenna clicked on her emails and stared at the article. She couldn't believe what she was reading. "He seriously wrote this?" she asked, tears streaming down her face.

"Yes," Abby replied. "What are you still doing here? GO!"

Jenna quickly pressed 'post' and ran out of the door.

Chapter Twenty-Eight

Dan was sat in the Grand Hotel as he had done so many times before. He remembered the first day he met Jenna: all full of arrogance towards her; he couldn't believe she said yes to him shadowing. He remembered how she looked when she rushed past him to the front desk and how embarrassed she was when she realised who he was.

He remembered how out of breath and stressed she was, the hair stuck to her face by the sweat. But he also remembered how she stormed out talking about dancing naked or something like that. He couldn't help but smile.

She wasn't his. Yet he was worried he'd lose her.

He stared once more at the door. If Abby had

shown her the article, Jenna would have made her decision as to whether she wanted to be with him or not.

Twenty minutes went past and his heart sank. She clearly wasn't coming. Devastated and lost, he bent down to pick up his coat when something ran into the side of him.

"Do you mind? I am actually standing her—" He stopped his sentence and looked right into Jenna's eyes. "You came?"

She smiled. Not one of those small smiles she used to do, but a beaming smile. One that couldn't be faked. One that writers only write about and people only see in movies. Her teeth glistened, but her tears still ran down her face.

"Shh," he said, holding onto her. "It's all OK."

"It's… It's more than OK," Jenna said. "All these years I've tried to save me from me. But it looks like all I ever needed was you."

Dan stroked her face and wiped her tears. He really had hit the jackpot with this woman. He couldn't believe his luck.

"No, dear. This is what you don't understand." Dan looked lovingly into her face. "It's you who saved me."

"I love you." Jenna smiled up at Dan.

"I love you too. Very, very much."

Helga, Lionel, Margot and Abby all stood in the doorway of the Grand Hotel hugging themselves. "What a happy ending," Lionel said to the group.

"Hear, hear," Abby, Helga and Margot chanted all at once.

They all giggled and left the love birds to their embrace.

Chapter Twenty-Nine

D ear Everyone,

I know things have been difficult lately, I am sure you have read a certain article in a certain magazine slaying my existence. Well, I have forgiven that person and I will tell you why.

I love him.

Yes, I know that is difficult to understand but I do. I love him with all my heart. What's more odd is that, I know he loves me. The hardest part of reading that article was knowing that those were his feelings and yet he wrote it.

But then, I was informed, he wrote it before he loved me. Yes, I know you could say that anyone can lie, but I know him and I know his loved ones and they don't lie.

I have helped so many of you in the past. So many of you have become my friends because I have helped you. I love you all so much. I thank you all for the support you have given me over the years. For standing by me despite my darkest times.

So like I said before, I forgive him. I forgive him for feeling that way in the past. I have changed, I was a different person when I wrote the book to now. All he could see was a shy person who was polar opposites of the person I am today. Truth be told, I saw him as arrogant and obnoxious and would have probably written something equally as nasty.

But, the main reason I have forgiven him is because he saw the error of his ways. He tried to make contact to explain. Something I was too dumb to accept and therefore I had done something to hurt him.

Where are we in a world where forgiveness isn't an option? We would be in a dark descent of hatred if that were true. Without love or forgiveness we become bitter and obstinate. We become enemies of ourselves and that was something I didn't want.

The final reason I forgave him was because I saw him forgive someone he loved, someone who he had lost before and I thought to myself: Jenna, if he can forgive them. I can forgive him for doing his job.

That was all it was: a job.

So to all you people out there who have lost or have been treated badly. Find some way to forgive them. They don't need to know it, you don't even have to show your forgiveness. But do it inside.

Because believe me, when you do. The whole world will open up, just for you.

A good friend once told me:

You can't live your life wondering about the tomorrow's of the world, just focus on today and how far you have come.

So that is what I will leave you with for now. Live for today, focus on your achievements and love like there is no tomorrow.

Love you guys always,

Jenna Pace

Five Years Later

*A*nd we are back, live at the Metro News with Ashleigh Jonathan.

"Ah! Margot, Lionel! It's back. It's back!" screeched Helga from the living room sofa. Margot charged into the living room with Lionel not far behind carrying the tea. "Quickly!" she urged as she pointed to the TV screen.

"I am so excited!" cried Margot, only to be shushed by Helga and Lionel, who had since sat by Helga and kissed her on the forehead.

"Now for our entertainment segment. You may have heard of the Watergate scandal, or even conspiracy theories on aliens. But everyone has heard about the love story of the journalist and his muse. Daniel and Jenna, welcome to the show." Ashleigh leered at Daniel and nodded at Jenna.

"Thank you," the happy couple smiled to the camera in unison. "We are so happy to be here," Jenna finished.

"Charmed," smirked Ashleigh. "So Jenna, the agony aunt and Daniel the journalist. An unlikely but beloved couple. Care to explain how this happened?"

Dan sighed. *Not another 'how did you meet?' question.* "Well, it is quite simple. I fell in love with an amazing and talented woman who was only ever herself and we were pulled apart by people only wanting to better themselves, not others, and we broke through." He smiled deeply into Jenna's face and kissed her forehead.

"Not on TV, Daniel," Helga reprimanded the screen, making Lionel snort.

"So you have decided to collaborate on a new book." Ashleigh diverted the conversation towards the hardback copy of a book in her hand. "Be True To Yourself, on shelves Monday 18th. What inspired you to write this?"

"Me!" giggled Lionel. Margot tutted in humour.

"Well that is a very good question, Ashleigh. The inspiration comes from all the people in our lives who taught us to be strong and were always themselves. We have many people in our lives who are true to themselves and we wouldn't have it any other way. But there are so many people out there, struggling and needing help that we thought…" Jenna's voice trailed off.

"We would help them express it," Dan finished, squeezing Jenna's hand. "The proceeds go to British Liver Trust for without them, my father wouldn't have had the transplant or support he desperately needed. He is recovering at the moment." Dan smiled.

Ashleigh gave a sympathetic smile. "Glad to hear it. So what is next? Autobiography? *Another* self-help book?"

"I don't like this woman," Margot huffed. "She seems stuffy."

Lionel grunted in agreement and Helga chuckled, "Maybe she should read the book," making the other two laugh.

Dan stood up as a result of the question, causing Ashleigh and Jenna to look at each other in confusion. "Well it is a good job you asked this, Ashleigh." He bent down on one knee towards Jenna.

"OH. MY. GOD!" yelled Lionel, Margot and Helga

as Ashleigh and Jenna both stared at Dan in shock.

Dan pulled out a small box from his pocket and began, "Jenna. My world starts and ends with you. From the moment I saw you, I knew you were special. We have both been through so much and I couldn't imagine a world where I am without you. So. Jenna Pace. Will you marry me?"

A few seconds went by of pure silence both on air and in Helga's living room. It seemed as though time had stood still as everyone held their breath waiting for a response.

"Dan…" Jenna's eyes filled up with tears, "Yes. Yes of course I will marry you," before jumping into his arms and crying.

Ashleigh, dumbfounded, looked at the camera, composed herself and announced, "Well you heard it here first, folks! Many congratulations to you both. And that is all we have time for tonight, thank you and enjoy your evening."

As the credits rolled the camera stayed focused on the happy couple as Dan placed the ring on Jenna's finger and spun her around in a tight embrace. Helga, Margot and Lionel pulled themselves into a tight hug.

Lionel looked around at his new life with Helga

and Margot before looking back at the screen. "Wow," he managed through tears of happiness. It truly felt like a magical end to their bumpy but life-changing journey.

****

A man was slumped in a grand chair of the penthouse suite in the Westminster Prestige, staring at the TV screen with disbelief whilst holding a whiskey to his temple.

He clicked his fingers and a woman in her 20s wandered over to him to top up his glass. On her wrist was a bandage and on her cheek, a cut.

"Remember to always keep my whisky flowing, OK gorgeous?" He grabbed the woman's face and stroked her cheek as she flinched.

Three years, he thought. *Three years I have been in rehab, trying to make my life right to win her back and when I am out... well, a blog with two editors, then a three-part book deal and now... marriage!*

Liam sneered at the TV before throwing his glass at the screen, shattering it all over the floor. The woman shrieked but Liam did not seem to notice.

"Clean that up!" he shouted. "And get me another whiskey!"

As the woman debated which to do first, Liam laughed. "If she thinks I will let her run away from me that easily... Our story is not over, Jenna. Far, far from it."

ABOUT THE AUTHOR

My name is Stephanie Francis. Writing has been a hobby of mine for years. I am very excited to see my book officially published and hope to see many more in the future.

I am a primary teacher, a chocoholic, and totally obsessed with puppies. I have two miniature schnauzer dogs called Teddy and Winnie who are awesome.

Family is very important to me and I wouldn't be who I am today without my mum and my grandparents (the latter I miss very much).

I am soon to be married to my amazing fiancé, Jake (who totally didn't bribe me with chocolate to write this… honest).

Printed in Poland
by Amazon Fulfillment
Poland Sp. z o.o., Wrocław

51278821R00105